D0360089

DATE DUE

			PRINTED IN U.S.A.

MYS

To Love *and* *to* Vanish

Tara Randel

Annie's®

AnniesFiction.com

Library of Congress-in-Publication Data
To Love and to Vanish / by Tara Randel
p. cm.
I. Title
                       2016944833

AnniesFiction.com
(800) 282-6643
Amish Inn Mysteries™
Series Creator: Shari Lohner
Series Editors: Lorie Jones and Shari Lohner
Cover Illustrator: Kelley McMorris

10 11 12 13 14 | Printed in China | 9 8 7 6 5 4 3 2 1

"Love bears all things, believes all things, hopes all things, endures all things."
−1 Corinthians 13:7

1

"Liz, wait up!"

Liz Eckardt turned to find Renee Paulson, the young bride-to-be, calling her name.

Smiling, Renee joined Liz as she headed inside the inn. "The party turned out great. Thank you."

The Paulson-Conrad rehearsal dinner taking place on the grounds of the Olde Mansion Inn, which was booked with wedding guests, was still going strong.

"I should thank *you*," Liz said. "I'm very happy you chose the inn for this party as well as your wedding ceremony and reception."

"How could I resist? Mary Ann kept reminding me how awesome this place is. She's pretty good PR."

Liz tucked her dark blond hair behind one ear. Her good friend Mary Ann Berne, godmother to Renee, had helped Renee plan her wedding and had suggested the inn for the location. Liz was thrilled to assist with the wedding preparations, and she didn't mind the added publicity her bed-and-breakfast would garner either.

"Josh and I can't think of a better place to say our vows, and the guests love it here too," Renee gushed, the flush of excitement coloring her cheeks.

Deep pride filled Liz. Owning the stately Victorian inn gave her great satisfaction. It was right on track financially, and reservations were steady. She loved hosting weddings, and this one held a special place in her heart because Renee was an important part of Mary Ann's life and Liz had spent many hours with the young woman. Mary Ann was co-owner of Sew Welcome, a fabric- and quilting-supply shop located on the ground floor of the inn, and Renee frequently visited.

Getting ready for the wedding had been exhausting, but the results were clearly what Renee had hoped for, so all the hard work was worth it. Liz had rented a huge tent for the rehearsal dinner and reception, and the vast canopy dominated most of the backyard. It had taken the guys from the rental company a few hours to set up the tent, lay a removable floor, and arrange the tables, which were decorated simply for tonight's dinner. Bright and early tomorrow morning, Liz and her friends would decorate for the ceremony and the reception.

"Tomorrow will be beautiful," Liz assured her. "When you and Josh exchange your vows, everyone will be wiping away happy tears."

The forecast called for a sunny October day, just as they'd hoped. The couple would stand under an arch strategically placed in front of Jaynes Lake. Liz could already picture the sun reflecting off the water, creating a breathtaking backdrop for the ceremony.

"That's the plan," Renee replied in her normal perky tone, brightness shining in her blue eyes. Her wavy blond hair curled about her shoulders, and she exuded the girl-next-door look. "But for now, the rowdy party isn't going to break up anytime soon."

"Let them stay as long as they like. Since all the inn guests are out here, I won't get any complaints about the noise."

Renee laughed, then stepped closer, folding Liz in a tight hug. "Your help, and Mary Ann's, means the world to me. Without both of you, I couldn't imagine my special day turning out any better than I know it will."

Liz returned the hug, reveling in the moment. This entire weekend, set aside to make Renee's dreams come true, was truly priceless. "We want you to have special memories," she murmured.

Renee pulled back, swiping at her eyes. "Josh and I could get married in a cave, and I'd still be happy. But this?" She gestured to the backyard. "Thank you."

"Enough of your thanks. Your wedding has been a joy to arrange. Now go focus on the big day."

Renee stood on her tiptoes and squealed, "I'm getting married!"

"Indeed you are." Liz chuckled at Renee's exuberance. It was contagious and heartwarming.

"I'm going to find Josh. Maybe we can get Mark to check his playlist for a wild dance number."

"Watch out. You know Sadie will be right there in the middle of the action."

"You'll join us?"

"I still have work to do." Liz waved her off. "Go. Enjoy."

Renee turned and danced her way back to the tent, her lovely apricot dress floating around her legs. Even in high heels, she easily waltzed over the neatly cut grass. Her bridal attendants surrounded her, giggling.

Sure enough, Sadie Schwarzentruber, the other owner of Sew Welcome, led the dance line. The smiling seventy-something wore a headband of glittering beads and waved her arms in the air. As usual, Sadie had the energy of a woman half her age, and her youthful enthusiasm rubbed off on everyone she encountered.

With Sadie in charge, I don't see this party ending before midnight. Shaking her head, Liz continued inside to check on the behind-the-scenes activity.

She entered the large kitchen to find the caterers had already cleaned up from the night's dinner and were prepping for the next day. At first Liz had balked at the idea of hiring caterers because she still held on to the can-do attitude that had served her well in her law career, her life before the inn. But Renee and Mary Ann told her she couldn't do it all, and she was pragmatic enough to realize they were right. Besides, Renee said she wanted Liz to enjoy the day, not see it flash by in a whirlwind of activity. After Renee's heartfelt hug, Liz was glad she'd agreed to hire help.

She quickly conferred with Tammy Potts, owner of Pleasant Creek Catering. Tammy had the hors d'oeuvres, lunch menu, and drinks covered for the noon wedding. Naomi Mason, Liz's good friend and owner of the local bakery, Sweet Everything, would provide the wedding cake and special desserts. Naomi was excited to participate in Renee's special day and promised a truly epic cake design. She'd even managed to keep it a secret from Sadie, which was a feat in itself.

Renee had also asked Mary Ann to make pies for the occasion. The woman was amazingly talented, and it was no wonder her pies won first prize at the county fair every year. Mary Ann couldn't refuse her goddaughter's plea and agreed to bake three different fruit pies.

Satisfied the catering staff had everything under control, Liz strode out of the kitchen. She noticed the groom alone in the four-season room, talking on his cell phone. Tall, with dark brown hair and eyes, Josh paced before the windows overlooking the festivities. Even from a distance, Liz picked up on his tight tone. Not wanting to eavesdrop, she waved, then stopped when Josh held up his hand and motioned her over.

"I told you what needs to be done. I don't want to have this conversation again." Josh hung up, the irritation on his face quickly transforming into easygoing charm. "Liz, do you have a minute?"

"Sure. What's up?"

"I have a request."

Surprised, Liz asked, "We didn't miss anything, did we?"

"No. Can you keep something for me until tomorrow?" Josh grinned, his eyes lighting up. "I have a present for Renee. I was wondering if you'd hold it until before the ceremony. I'm afraid I might forget it in all the activity."

"How sweet. Of course."

"I would have handed the gift to Mary Ann, but every time I try to talk to her, Renee pops up."

"I'll tell Mary Ann your intention and let her give the present to Renee."

"Great. I'll run out to the car and get it."

A few minutes later he returned with a small, silver gift-wrapped box. "It's a brooch my grandmother wore on her wedding day, given to her by her mother. My mother wore it too, and I want to keep the tradition going. I'm hoping Renee will feel like part of the family by wearing this heirloom."

"Renee will be thrilled."

"Since I haven't seen her dress, I'm not sure where the brooch will go, but I trust you and Mary Ann will figure it out."

"Yes, that's what we women do."

"I didn't mean to come off like a clueless male, but in this case, I am." He laughed. "I don't get having to find the perfect dress or the secrecy once it's purchased. And then there are the bridesmaids' dresses. All I know is the color scheme Renee settled on months ago."

Liz laughed with him. "There are some things that are timeless, like shopping for the bridal gown and the hours the bride spends getting ready for the ceremony. Don't worry. We'll find the perfect place to show off the brooch."

Josh let out a long breath. "I have to admit, the stress has finally gotten to me. I had no idea so much time and planning go into a wedding. I'm looking forward to tomorrow—and to the vacation afterward even more. I need a break from work. Spending two weeks in the Caribbean with Renee is the perfect way to wind down." He must have realized how that sounded because his face suddenly colored. "Don't get me wrong. I know this is everything Renee has dreamed of, but . . ."

"I understand. You're looking forward to the honeymoon. No need to explain. Promise me you'll take a deep breath and relax tomorrow."

"I can't imagine spending my life with anyone but Renee, so yeah, I'll make sure I slow down and focus."

Liz patted him on the arm. "Go on outside. Sounds like one of your friends turned up the dance music."

"You don't mind the commotion?"

"It's a party."

"See you tomorrow." Josh gave her a jaunty salute and disappeared out the back door.

Liz took the gift to her private quarters. Like Josh, she didn't want the box misplaced in the whirlwind events of the morning. And once the girls showed up bright and early to get dressed for the wedding, things were bound to get hectic.

She'd just closed the door to her room when a group of chatting women descended upon her. Mary Ann, Sadie, Naomi, Caitlyn Ross, and Opal Ringenberg were members of a long-standing quilting group called the Material Girls. Sadie, Mary Ann, and Opal were in their sixties and seventies, Liz and Naomi in their forties, and Caitlyn a busy twenty-something. The age range didn't matter; they were tight-knit and true friends. When they'd welcomed Liz into the fold, she'd been honored. Truth be told, she still was.

"Liz, we need to wrap our gift for the kids," Sadie announced in her no-nonsense tone.

Mary Ann brought up the rear, brushing back her neatly bobbed silver hair, her smile a bit melancholy considering the circumstances.

Liz waited until the others passed, then joined her. "Problem?"

"No. Just wishing Janey were here."

Janey Paulson had been Mary Ann's best friend growing up. They'd shared everything from family secrets to schoolwork and crushes on boys. They'd been each other's maid of honor and godmother to each other's children and grandchildren. Renee's parents were killed in a car accident when Renee was a child, and she had lived with her grandmother until Janey succumbed to cancer when Renee was sixteen. Mary Ann had taken over in the mother department, and although she and Renee were close, nothing took the place of family.

"Janey would be proud of Renee."

Mary Ann sniffed. "Yes, she would. I'm thankful to be part of Renee's life."

"She feels the same way."

They joined the other women and entered Sew Welcome. On the sales counter sat a huge box. The group moved forward to gaze at their newest creation nestled in thin silver tissue paper inside. The bright overhead light cast an ethereal glow over the white, black, and silver fabric.

"This is the most beautiful quilt we've ever stitched together," Liz stated with proud satisfaction.

In the center of the quilt top was an image of Renee and Josh inside a heart, surrounded by a small, dark border. The remainder of the quilt contained squares of fabric that came from their childhoods.

"Renee will be pleased." Mary Ann placed her hand over her heart. "I can't believe my goddaughter is getting married."

Opal touched the fabric. "Mary Ann, it's amazing you held on to that box of Janey's fabric and Renee's baby clothes all these years. Adding pieces to the quilt from Renee's grandmother makes the gift much more special."

Caitlyn grinned. "Especially since it's a surprise. She has no idea you kept the material."

"I always knew the fabric would come in handy someday. I'd hoped to use it for Renee's wedding and when she has children."

"With Josh's mom giving us fabric from when he was a little boy," Sadie said, "the entire design came out precisely as we planned."

Liz shot Sadie an amused look. "Like *we* planned? You came up with the pattern. It's one of a kind."

"I'm still amazed you figured out how to transfer the image of Renee and Josh from a photo onto the fabric," Caitlyn said in awe.

Sadie shrugged. "It was nothing. You can find all kinds of instructions on the Internet."

"Still," Opal said, "it's original, just like you."

"Yes, but we worked on it together, so it's a group effort."

Liz couldn't get over how generous these talented women were. Sadie could probably publish a book of her creative designs. Mary Ann excelled at placement and stitching the finished product. Their collective expertise drew quilting enthusiasts from around the country to Sew Welcome.

"This quilt was created with special love," Mary Ann added, her voice thick. "Not every gift can make that claim."

"And to think we almost decided to give the couple a set of china," Sadie said in exasperation. "Really. Owners of a quilt store not sewing a unique quilt for the occasion?"

The women stood around the counter admiring their creation, then placed the top on the box. Naomi and Liz rolled out glittery wedding paper from a roll, Opal cut it, and Caitlyn squared off the edges and applied tape. Mary Ann finished the project by affixing a big bow.

They were storing the supplies when a knock sounded.

Liz looked up to see Tammy hovering in the doorway.

"Liz, I have one last matter to discuss with you before I head home," the caterer said.

"Be right there." Liz faced the group. "Everyone remembers their part for tomorrow?"

Sadie pointed at the present. "Make sure this box gets to the gift table."

Caitlyn nodded. "Opal and I are on decorating duty. We'll be here at nine."

"The baking is under control," Naomi assured them. "Liz, I'm going to bring my dress when I deliver the cake. Do you mind if I change in your quarters?"

"Not at all. And I'll make sure the guests have a good breakfast before the ceremony. Looks like we're covered."

Mary Ann smiled. "I can't thank you enough. Helping Renee plan this wedding has been wonderful, but to have my good friends rally around . . . I must say, I'm touched." She held up crossed fingers. "Here's to tomorrow going off without a hitch."

2

Chaos reigned in the library the next morning. Liz carried in a plate of fresh cranberry muffins left over from breakfast, thinking the girls might enjoy the treat.

Dresses hung from a movable rack. Makeup containers covered the top of an antique desk. Gold strappy sandals were lined up before the fireplace. Fresh floral bouquets, delivered earlier by the florist, scented the room. Before long the photographer would be knocking on the door, ready to take candid shots of the bride and her attendants.

"This is more than I expected," Liz whispered to Mary Ann. "Are we sure there are only five women in here besides us?"

"Ceremony jitters."

"Serving this morning's breakfast went off with less drama."

"That's because you and Sarah are used to taking such good care of your guests."

"True." Sarah Borkholder had assisted Liz with breakfast, and later, during the ceremony, Sarah would tidy up the rooms and clean the bathrooms.

Renee hurried over, wrapped up in a robe, her hair in fat curlers. "Tell me this is normal."

Mary Ann took hold of her hand. "Absolutely. Enjoy it."

"How?" The bride-to-be's hands fluttered in dismay. "We should be dressed by now, our guests are arriving, and I can't remember the vows I wrote for the ceremony."

Liz ushered Renee across the room, then clapped. "Attention, ladies. Time to put on your dresses." She checked the time on the grandfather clock. "You have fifteen minutes."

A shout went up among the women.

Renee shot Liz a look. "That was supposed to help?"

"What can I say? I'm new at this."

Renee unzipped the garment bag protecting her flowing white gown. "There's more commotion going on here than in my kindergarten classroom."

"Wait. I have to give you something first." Liz stepped over to the bookshelf where she'd placed Josh's gift earlier. She passed the wrapped box to Mary Ann.

Mary Ann placed it in Renee's hands. "Courtesy of your groom."

"Oh." Renee sank onto the nearest chair, holding the box as if it were a precious artifact.

"Aren't you going to open it?" Mary Ann questioned with a tilt of her head.

"I don't . . . I didn't expect this. We talked about it and decided not to give each other gifts."

Liz gestured toward the box. "Go ahead. I think you'll understand when you open it."

The other girls gathered around to watch the unveiling of Josh's gift.

Renee untied the bow and removed the paper, revealing a midnight-blue velvet box.

The tiny hinges on the box squeaked when she lifted the top. Nestled inside on white satin was a sapphire framed by an intricate silver filigree design.

Renee gasped. "This is the Conrad brooch. Josh told me about it."

Mary Ann beamed. "He wanted you to carry on the family tradition of wearing it on your wedding day."

"There's your something old and something blue," one of the bridesmaids said.

Renee traced the stone with her finger. When she looked up, tears sparkled in her eyes. "I love Josh so much." She took her cell phone from the end table. "I know we agreed not to talk this morning, but I have to let him know I love his gift."

The other girls sighed and murmured to each other until Liz reminded them they needed to get dressed.

"Your grandmother would have loved all this." Mary Ann hugged Renee.

"I know she's grateful you're here on my big day."

Mary Ann stepped back. "Where else would I be?"

Soon the bridesmaids were dressed in persimmon-colored, sleeveless chiffon dresses and short lace jackets in the same shade. The bride, beautiful in a floor-length, slim-fitting lace gown, with seed pearls sewn into the bodice and long sleeves ending in points that extended beyond her wrists, smiled at the group. Her hair had been pulled back, so she could don the shoulder-length veil with beading around the edges.

Liz let the antsy photographer in, and the next wedding-day tradition began.

"I'm going to check on Opal and Caitlyn's decorating progress," Liz whispered in Mary Ann's ear before slipping from the room.

The caterers hustled about the kitchen, so Liz bypassed them to step outside. As predicted, the noon wedding would be celebrated under sunny skies with a nip in the air. As she headed to the tent, she scoped out the yard. Her other employee, Kiera Williams, had spent the last few weeks whipping the grounds into shape, and by the look of the foliage, resplendent in autumn colors, her diligent care had paid off. The scrappy teenager loved working outdoors and had a gift when it came to flowers and plants. Liz was fortunate to have two reliable young women working at the inn.

Liz continued to the tent. Rows of chairs covered in ivory with persimmon-colored bows tied behind each one faced the decorated arch beside the lake. A long white runner waited to be rolled out to create a center aisle for the wedding procession. "Great job, ladies."

Caitlyn spun around, her short, red-streaked hair shining bright in the sunlight. "Good timing too. Guests are starting to arrive."

Liz glanced around the reception area. The tables were covered in ivory linens. The centerpieces consisted of tall hurricane glasses with chunky yellow candles inside. Surrounding the glasses were vines of red, brown, and orange berries. The decor was simple yet elegant for the noon wedding.

"Everything is exactly as the bride ordered," Liz stated, satisfaction settling deep within her.

"Speaking of the bride," Opal said, "have the nerves kicked in yet?"

"A bit. She's ready to say her vows and become Josh's wife."

"His folks arrived," Caitlyn pointed out. "I've never seen them this happy. Or the judge smile so much."

Judge Conrad's serious-minded reputation preceded him, no matter the event.

"Today he deserves to let his guard down," Opal said.

Liz agreed. This was a big day for the Conrads' only son. "Are the groomsmen ready to take their places?"

"I think so. I saw them earlier when they drove up. Apparently, they're hanging out on the front porch until it's time for the ceremony."

"And Josh? How's he holding up?"

Caitlyn tilted her head. "I didn't see him, but I bet he's around somewhere, pacing off his nerves."

"He was overwhelmed when I spoke to him last night," Liz said. "Maybe now that he's only minutes away from becoming a married man, he's calmed down."

"Does that ever happen to a single guy?" Caitlyn teased.

"My George was more excited about our wedding than I was," Opal admitted. "I never told you, but he planned the entire thing."

"*Your* George?"

"I know. Hard to imagine. But back then, he was impulsive and romantic. All I can say is, he could tear up the dance floor."

Liz exchanged an amused look with Caitlyn. "The same George who loves to sit at home and watch train documentaries?"

"Yes." Opal lifted her chin. "He's mellowed with age."

"Please tell me he'll be at the reception," Caitlyn begged. "I have to see you two dancing together."

"He was going to come, but since I got here early to help, he bowed out."

"Rats."

Opal grinned.

Sadie breezed into the tent. "Enough chitchat. I need to get a few more pictures." She held up her new phone and snapped a shot of the women.

"You're a menace with that thing," Caitlyn responded. "How many pictures did you take last night?"

"I lost count." Sadie set down the phone. "But not as many as I plan on taking today."

Liz chuckled. "Then we'd better finish. It's almost noon."

The women quickly wrapped up loose ends.

Pastor Brad from Pleasant Creek Community Church arrived, and Liz met him by the arch.

"How are we doing on time?" he asked.

"We're right on schedule. The bride is ready. I haven't seen Josh yet, but he's around here somewhere." She waved at Mary Ann who had popped her head out the side door of the inn.

Mary Ann returned the wave with a thumbs-up and disappeared back inside.

"Looks like it's time to get a certain young couple married."

Guests streamed into the yard and were ushered to their seats. Pastor Brad stood under the arch, a serene smile on his face. When the groomsmen hadn't taken their places, Liz decided they needed a little prodding.

As she walked around the side of the inn, she nearly ran into Naomi and a young girl who worked at the bakery. They carried a round, three-tiered cake. The ivory fondant was sculpted in a quilted pattern, with silver beads at the cross point of each square. A collection of yellow roses adorned the top layer.

Liz pulled up short, avoiding disaster.

Naomi's wide-eyed gaze met hers. "That would have been bad."

"DEFCON 1 bad," Liz agreed.

"We're running a bit late," Naomi said, a frazzled look on her face. "I'll explain later." She carefully continued on with her assistant.

Blowing out a breath, Liz climbed the porch steps to find the four groomsmen standing in a huddle. "Are you guys ready?"

They glanced at each other but did not answer.

"Problem, gentlemen?"

Mark, the best man, stammered, "Um, not sure."

"Where's Josh?"

"He was supposed to meet us out here, but he hasn't shown up yet."

"Do you know where he is?"

Mark adjusted his bow tie. "When I talked to him early this morning he said he was coming to the inn way before us. Maybe he's inside."

"Let me check." Liz rushed inside, nearly tripping over her resident bulldog, Beans, sprawled on the floor. She searched the downstairs rooms, avoiding the library. She didn't want to worry Renee, and besides, Josh wouldn't be there anyway. Then she climbed the stairs and knocked on the doors to the guest rooms. No answers. Puzzled, she turned to go back downstairs and nearly collided with Sarah. "Have you seen Josh?"

Sarah wore her usual modest gray dress and apron with her hair pulled under a black *Kapp* and carried a laundry basket of towels. "No. Everyone left for the ceremony. The rooms are empty."

"The guys haven't seen him. They thought he was calming his nerves inside."

Sarah looked bewildered. "I have not seen him."

Liz returned to the front porch. Concern twisted into dread when Mark faced her, his forehead creased with worry. "I called Josh a bunch of times. No answer."

"Did he have any last-minute errands?"

"Not that I know of."

"Odd. Perhaps something came up concerning the wedding."

Not one of the guys could come up with a reason for Josh not being there.

"Let me talk to his folks."

The parents of the groom were waiting in the four-season room until it was time to walk down the aisle. From the windows, they had a bird's-eye view of the guests arriving and being shown to their seats.

Judge Conrad, dressed in a tuxedo, ran his hand over his balding head. His wife, Elyse, decked out in a lovely designer dress with her dark hair professionally styled, straightened his bow tie. Liz hated to disturb the intimate moment. Nevertheless, she caught the eye of Josh's dad and waved him over.

When the judge joined her, she steered him to the far side of the room. "Quick question. Did Josh have any stops to make before the wedding?"

"No. He took care of all the details yesterday."

"Did you see him this morning?"

"Very early. He wanted to get here before the others."

"So he was excited?"

"Why so many questions?" The judge's no-nonsense tone rattled Liz. She never wanted to face him in court.

"The groomsmen can't take their places until the groom arrives."

"Arrives?" The judge's voice rose. "He's not here?"

"I'm not certain. No one has seen him."

Judge Conrad pulled his cell phone from his inside jacket pocket. He thumbed in a command and put the phone to his ear. "Voice mail."

"Darling," Mrs. Conrad said as she approached, "what's the holdup?"

The judge shot Liz a warning look and said, "You know how these things go, dear. I'm going to check on Josh."

His wife patted his arm.

"This could all be a mistake," Liz said as they walked through the downstairs hallway toward the front porch.

"My son will be here," the judge assured her. Or was he trying to convince himself?

As they went out the front door, Mark stepped forward. "We checked the parking lot and the street. No sign of Josh's car."

"Which is weird," another young man said. "We were supposed to decorate it during the reception."

"This is very unsettling," the judge muttered. "We must do something."

Almost in unison, all the men on the porch took out their cell phones.

"No return call."

"No texts."

"He isn't answering."

Liz placed a hand over her swirling stomach. *This is not good.* "Is there a place Josh might go? Maybe he needed to clear his head and lost track of time."

"Usually he goes to see Renee when things are bothering him," Mark said.

"That wouldn't work this morning."

"Josh's friend Caleb Hoffner lives on a farm outside of town. There are no phones or distractions out there, and sometimes Josh visits him for the quiet."

With the Amish community being a vital part of Pleasant Creek, it made sense that Josh had a friend there, someone not caught up in the hubbub of modern living.

"Caleb is supposed to come to the wedding, but I haven't seen him either," another groomsman said. "Want me to drive out to the farm and see if there's a problem?"

Liz glanced at the judge, waiting for his lead. His normally healthy skin color had faded to a sickly gray, and his chest rose on a deep breath. "Yes. Before we jump to conclusions, head out that way. Maybe he had car trouble."

The groomsman took off.

"How do you want to handle this?" Liz asked the judge. "The ceremony was supposed to start five minutes ago."

"First, let's not panic. There's probably a reasonable explanation for Josh being late."

"We can tell the guests we're running behind, but what about Renee? She's going to wonder what the delay is."

"Stall," the judge said as he stalked back into the inn.

"How am I supposed to do that?" Liz asked the group standing in front of her.

The three men staring at her didn't answer.

She needed to think. The wedding at her inn must proceed without any problems. She'd promised Renee a perfect day. Okay, she'd been in dicier spots than this one before, so she could handle it. All she had to do was keep everyone calm until Josh showed up.

New plan: Stall and keep calm.

Liz heard rapid footsteps in the foyer, and then the door flew open.

Renee stepped onto the porch, her face pale, her eyes wide.

Liz noticed the brooch, pinned on the sash at Renee's waist, and dread enveloped her.

"Where's Josh?" Renee cried, glancing around in search of her groom.

Liz looked at the silent group, then back at the bride. So much for stalling until they had answers. "Renee, we need to talk."

3

Liz pointed Renee back toward the library, then faced the groomsmen. She spoke softly. "How did she know?"

One of the men shifted uncomfortably. "I might have texted her."

"Might have?" Liz rolled her eyes. "As of right now, no texts, no Facebook updates, no Twitter. We are officially on lockdown." Right, like that would hold them off, but she had to put her foot down for Renee's sake.

Darting inside, she fell in step behind Renee. After her outburst on the porch, the young woman didn't speak at all. As soon as they entered the library, everyone turned to them.

Mary Ann rushed over, frowning as she took in Renee's pale face and Liz's serious expression. "What's wrong?"

"It's Josh." Liz glanced at Renee, concerned by her stillness. "He seems to be missing."

"He never texted me back." Renee shook her head. "I thought it was because we'd agreed not to be in touch until we met under the arch, but now . . ."

As the bridesmaids circled Renee, Liz led Mary Ann to the other side of the room.

Mary Ann stared Liz down. "What's going on? Don't sugarcoat."

"I'm not. We really don't know anything yet."

"Except Josh isn't here."

"Right. One of the groomsmen went looking for him, and Judge Conrad is aware of the situation."

Mary Ann glanced at the group of women. They spoke quietly, their bewilderment evident. "The day was supposed to go off without a hitch. How could this happen?"

"Josh is only a few minutes late. Maybe he's on—"

"Mary Ann?" Renee's reedy voice carried from across the room. She hurried over, Liz on her heels.

Still pale, Renee straightened her back and said, "Josh would never stand me up."

"We don't know that's the case."

Renee concentrated on the phone in her hand. "He still isn't answering. It's not like him to keep me hanging." She blinked, as though suddenly jolted from her thoughts. "The guests. What will we tell them?"

Liz stepped forward. "Nothing. I'll fill Pastor Brad in on the situation. We'll stall until Josh gets here."

Relief washed over Renee's face.

Liz left the room and paused with her hand still on the doorknob. This was a first. She'd never attended a wedding where the groom went AWOL. What was the protocol?

"Hey, what's going on?" Naomi asked as she exited Liz's quarters, having changed into her dress and styled her dark, curly hair. "Shouldn't we be seated with everyone else?"

"Slight change of plans."

"What do you mean?"

"We hit a snag."

"Bride got cold feet?"

"No. Renee's ready."

"Josh?" Naomi exclaimed. "No way!"

"I'm not saying he got cold feet, but . . ."

"He's not here?"

"Bingo."

"How horrible for Renee."

"Until we have more details we can't say anything. I'm going to speak to the pastor, and hopefully by then Josh will show up."

"What can I do?"

"Let the caterers know we might be running a little behind schedule."

"Got it."

"I'll be outside if you need me."

The two women went in opposite directions.

Judge Conrad stopped Liz in the backyard. "This isn't like Josh. No one can reach him."

The uneasiness Liz had tried to ignore returned twofold when she viewed the judge's stricken face. "Why don't you go inside and talk to Mrs. Conrad? I'll take care of matters."

"It's not your place. I should be the one handling the situation."

"I'm not the one missing a son." Liz gently pushed him toward the inn.

Ensuring the judge listened to her advice, she waited until he closed the door before seeking out Pastor Brad. In full innkeeper mode, she greeted friends and wedding guests along the way. Dressed to the nines in a navy blue dress and a beautiful derby hat to match, Sadie sat a few rows from the front with Opal and Caitlyn and sent her a curious look. Liz nodded, hoping that was enough to keep her friends from leaving their seats to ask questions. Once that happened, the crowd would know something was very wrong.

"Pastor Brad?"

"Is it the bride or the groom?"

Liz stopped short. "I beg your pardon?"

"Who didn't show up?"

Liz lowered her voice. "The groom. How did you know?"

"I've seen that same worried expression more than a few times."

"I'm not sure what to do."

Before he had a chance to answer, Judge and Mrs. Conrad walked hand in hand up the center aisle.

"This can't be good," Liz muttered.

"Usually isn't," he agreed.

Liz and the pastor stepped aside, letting the parents take center stage.

Sadie held up her new cell phone, ready to start documenting the wedding with pictures.

The judge cleared his throat. "I'm afraid we have to postpone the wedding."

A gasp rose from the crowd, followed by a barrage of questions.

The judge held up his hand. "The hors d'oeuvres will be served. Please visit until we have further information." With that, the couple headed back to the inn.

Guests rose, looking confused.

"Why don't we all move to the tent?" Sadie suggested. "I'm sure we'll know more soon."

Would they? Liz could only hope Sadie's words were true.

———————— ///////////////////////// ————————

By late afternoon, Josh still hadn't turned up.

He hadn't returned phone calls or texts. He hadn't been spotted around town, nor had anyone caught a glimpse of his silver Honda. No one at Caleb's farm or in the local Amish community had seen him or even Caleb for that matter. The judge finally broke down and called in Police Chief Houghton.

The guests milled around for a while, but no one ate the prepared food. The gravity of the situation was not lost on them.

Renee had been stood up at the altar.

"This is the worst thing ever." Opal and the Material Girls, minus Mary Ann who was comforting Renee, cleaned up as the last guests left.

"This is why I'm not having a wedding," Caitlyn informed them. "Eloping is easier and less stressful."

"But you'd miss out on a ceremony with family and friends wishing you happiness." Naomi smiled. "I couldn't imagine giving it up."

Caitlyn gestured at the empty tent. "Here's why."

"Planning a wedding can't be that bad," Liz said. True, she'd never been married, and her ex-boyfriend was an ex for good reason. "I may not have a great track record, but even I wouldn't want to miss out on the festivities."

"I've been to many weddings," Sadie said with sage wisdom. "This doesn't happen as often as you think."

"Still, why take a chance?" Caitlyn carefully removed a centerpiece from a table.

"Because love is worth it," Sadie said with conviction, as if she had the final word on the subject.

"I sure hope Renee feels the same way in a few days," Opal said. "What was Josh thinking?"

"That's the problem." Liz leaned against a nearby table. "We don't know. He certainly didn't seem to be dreading the wedding."

"He told me he loved me and couldn't wait to get married."

Liz whirled around to find Renee and Mary Ann joining the group. In unison, the other women faced the jilted bride.

Renee had changed out of her wedding gown into jeans and a pink T-shirt. Her hair was pulled back, her face free of makeup. Her red-rimmed eyes revealed the misery she tried to hide. In the late-afternoon sun, her young face appeared more ashen than ever.

"Renee wanted some fresh air," Mary Ann explained.

Renee gazed around the area, looking wistful. Not all the decorations had been removed yet. "This really turned out beautiful."

Sadie walked over and hugged Renee. "You have exceptional taste, my dear."

"I thought I did."

"Until you speak to Josh, don't give up."

Renee backed away from Sadie and threw her hands up. "How can I do that?"

"Josh is a good man," Mary Ann said quietly. "There must be a solid reason for him not being here."

"Or not contacting you," Opal added.

Taking a bracing breath, Renee focused on the group. "Please sit."

Liz didn't like the sudden determination on Renee's face, but she sat down with the others.

"I told you I needed some air," Renee said to Mary Ann, "but that's not the truth." She scanned the group, meeting each woman's curious gaze. "When I found out you were all still here, I wanted to talk to you."

"Go on," Mary Ann urged.

"The chief can't do much right now. Josh isn't officially a missing person yet. Once he is, I don't know if the police will even be able to find him. Lots of people, especially people the judge knows, are trying to locate Josh, and I appreciate it." With a shaky hand, Renee pulled out a chair and sat. "I trust all of you. Mary Ann, you've been a mom to me. And the rest of you have welcomed me into the quilting group from time to time." She paused. "So I want you to help me find out what happened to Josh."

Opal reached over to pat Renee's knee. "We aren't the police."

"No, but you've been known to get involved in a mystery or two. This . . . situation is no different."

"She makes an excellent argument," Sadie chimed in. "We *have* helped out a time or two."

Liz held back a grimace. *Helped* was too mild a word for the way they'd assisted others in Pleasant Creek.

"What makes you think the chief won't be successful?" Mary Ann asked.

"He has other obligations, even if Josh's case is his first priority."

"Doesn't mean he won't be diligent."

For the first time, a glimmer of hope shone in Renee's eyes. "But he won't be as invested as you are. And when things get personal, you ladies get to work."

"Get to work how?" Opal asked.

"Ask questions. Dig around for answers."

"We are good at asking questions," Sadie boasted.

"And bothering people in the process," Liz pointed out.

Renee slumped in the chair.

Liz wanted to bite her tongue. "Not that we won't do it."

"You will?"

Liz looked to the group for confirmation. "Well, at least I will."

"Count me in," said Mary Ann, followed by affirmative reactions from the rest of the group.

Renee brushed at a loose strand of hair. "This is the first time I feel like something good might come out of this mess."

"We'll put our heads together," Sadie assured her.

"If Josh is okay . . ." Renee stopped, her voice thick. She swallowed. "I can't believe he just up and left. And if he didn't leave on his own, it means something has happened to him. Something he has no control over."

Renee's comment grabbed Liz's attention. "Did Josh have problems with anyone?"

"No. He's so easygoing."

Sadie perked up. "Why do you ask, Liz?"

"It may be nothing, but last night during the rehearsal dinner I came across Josh in the four-season room. He was on the phone, and although I only heard the tail end of the conversation, it sounded pretty heated."

"What did he say?" Caitlyn asked.

Liz closed her eyes and thought back. "He said something about doing what needed to be done and that he didn't want to have the conversation again." Her eyes popped open. "Once he saw me he hung up. Then he asked me to hold on to the box with the brooch until this morning. But . . ."

"What?" Sadie prompted.

"He said he was looking forward to the honeymoon and he needed a break from work."

Mary Ann took Renee's hand. "Any idea who he might have been speaking to?"

"No. But then, Josh doesn't like to worry me." She wrinkled her nose. "If we had only one argument, it was about him protecting me all the time. I asked him to stop. I wanted into this marriage on equal footing, and I told him exactly how I felt."

"How about a coworker or a client?" Naomi asked, moving the conversation in a less personal direction.

"I'm not sure. He doesn't usually have problems with anyone at work."

"Usually?" Liz asked.

"Well, he is a loan officer." Renee shrugged. "Sometimes he tells me about foreclosures or people having problems paying their debts, but he never mentions names."

After Liz's glimpse of Josh under pressure, she wondered if there was more happening than he'd let on.

"Come to think of it," Renee said, "the closer we got to the wedding date, the less he talked about work, but he was kind of uptight. Whatever he had going on, he kept to himself."

"So there was trouble?" Liz prodded.

Renee rubbed her temples. "Sorry. I don't know."

"No worries." Sadie smiled at Renee. "We'll find out one way or another."

Liz stood. "For now, let's put the decorations away. I don't know about you, but I think better when I'm busy."

"If you don't mind, I'm going to take Renee to my house."

"Mary Ann, you don't have to," Renee argued.

"Nonsense. You can't spend the night in your apartment alone. Besides, I want to."

Renee wavered for only a moment. "I'd like that."

Mary Ann placed her arm around Renee, and the two walked away.

Naomi picked up a napkin and wiped her eyes. "Poor thing."

Liz stopped folding a tablecloth. "Listen, we agreed to help Renee find Josh, but I wasn't just telling her what she needed to hear. We mean it, right?"

"Most certainly." Sadie gathered a centerpiece. "We have to try. For Renee's sake."

"Good." Liz finished her task. "I wanted to make sure we're all on the same page."

Caitlyn lifted a floral arrangement, then suddenly put it down. "Why didn't I think of this sooner?" She ran to her purse, dug out her cell phone, and furiously tapped on the display screen.

"Caitlyn?"

She held up one finger. "Hi, Marie? Caitlyn. Have any twentyish males come into the ER today?" She gave Josh's name and description. "Thanks. See you tomorrow." She ended the call. "No one fitting Josh's description has been in the ER."

Naomi exhaled. "We can be thankful for small favors."

"Maybe not." Sadie motioned toward the inn. "Here comes the police chief, and by the look of it, he has his business face on."

4

"Ladies." Stan Houghton, the rock-steady chief of the Pleasant Creek Police Department, approached them. With his gray hair and soothing smile, the chief appeared fatherly, but Liz had had dealings with the man and knew him to be fair yet shrewd.

Liz greeted him. "Any news about Josh?"

"I'm afraid not. I spoke to Judge Conrad earlier and Renee just a few minutes ago. I wanted to touch base with you, Liz."

"Is Josh considered missing?"

"Not yet. I'm only checking into the matter as a courtesy to the judge."

Made sense. Liz had never seen the judge this rattled before. Having a missing child, no matter his age, would do that to a parent.

The chief pulled out his smartphone to review his notes. "Liz, Renee told me you spoke to Josh last night about the wedding."

Right to the point. "Yes. He handed me a gift to give to Renee."

"A brooch?"

"Correct."

He scrolled through his phone. "He also spoke to you about work?"

"Not specifically. He mentioned looking forward to getting away for a while."

"And you heard him talking on his cell phone. What was his mood?"

"Stressed," Liz replied. "Maybe a bit angry. Or upset, anyway."

The chief typed in the information. "Anyone else have something to add?"

None of the other ladies had spoken to Josh, so the answer was no.

Houghton slid the phone into his uniform shirt pocket, his expression grave. "Did any of you see strangers hanging around the inn or the parking lot? People who might not have been invited to the wedding?"

Liz's stomach dipped. "Why?"

He shot her a warning look. "I'm asking the questions."

"No, but I was busy with the inn guests and then the bride," Liz responded. "We only got involved when we realized Josh wasn't here."

"Did you see Josh's car parked nearby?"

"I didn't check, but the groomsmen said they couldn't locate his car."

The lawman studied all the women. "Anyone else?"

Again, a resounding no.

"Is there a problem I need to know about, Chief?" Liz inquired. "I still have guests staying at the inn."

"I'm aware." He paused. "People, especially young men like Josh, simply don't up and disappear on their wedding day without good cause."

"Will you be making this a police matter?" Sadie asked.

Instead of answering her question, the chief said, "Thank you for your time." He turned on his heel and strode away.

"So much for knowing what's going on," Sadie grumbled. "I don't know about you, but I'm ready to go home."

"Me too. George will be waiting." Opal collected her purse.

"Need any more help?" Caitlyn asked Liz.

Liz gazed around the tent. "I think we're finished. The flower arrangements will be okay out here tonight. I just need to carry in the linens and decorations."

"I'll help," Naomi offered.

After the three women left, Liz and Naomi gathered up everything and headed inside.

"What a day." Naomi sighed. "Who would have ever thought Renee would go home tonight still single."

"Not anyone who knows them." Liz placed the linens on the counter as they passed through the utility room. "I guess you never really know what's going on with another person, no matter how close you are."

"If Josh took off, he kept his intentions quiet. Everyone was surprised."

"Wait. What happens to the wedding cake?"

Naomi frowned. "I suppose I'll keep it refrigerated for a few days. After that, I can either give it away or toss it."

"After all your hard work?"

"I may not like getting rid of it, but I wasn't the one stood up at the altar. That's so much worse."

"I know you. You're hoping Josh shows up with a reasonable explanation and the wedding goes on as planned."

"Is it that obvious?"

"For someone who wears her heart on her sleeve, yes."

"I bake every day, so it's not the work that went into making the cake that bothers me. It's the sentiment behind what the cake means and now . . ."

"Now it's not needed."

"Worse than not needed. More like destroyed."

"You'd think the idea of a runaway groom wouldn't affect us two single ladies this much, but my heart breaks for Renee." Liz brushed away tears. "I wish we knew what was going on with Josh."

"Maybe Renee will remember something else tomorrow."

The phone rang as Liz led the way into the kitchen. "Oh, boy. Word must be out about the canceled wedding. I hope this isn't a busybody looking for details."

"You could ignore it."

"I could, but it's the inn line." She picked up the handset. "Olde Mansion Inn."

"Liz." Mary Ann sounded breathless. "Do me a favor and check the library for the Conrad brooch."

Liz's eyes went wide as she met Naomi's gaze. "Why?"

"Renee can't find it. She thinks she might have misplaced it."

"Hold on." Liz set the handset on the counter, then turned to Naomi. "Come on. We need to search the library for the Conrad brooch."

"Renee left it here?"

"Not on purpose."

A few minutes later Naomi found the brooch on the floor behind a chair. "Got it." She held it up. "Renee must have dropped it when she removed her gown."

"Thank goodness." Liz ran back to the phone with the good news.

"Renee has been beside herself with worry," Mary Ann said. "On top of a truly horrible day, she couldn't imagine losing the brooch too."

"Tell her it's safe and sound."

"Actually, would you do me another favor?"

"Of course."

"Could you take it over to the Conrads' house? Renee will feel better knowing it's in their hands."

"Sure. It's quiet here. The guests are in their rooms, and Naomi and I were just talking."

"Thanks, Liz. Renee burst into tears as soon as we got home, so knowing you'll take care of the brooch will be a load off her mind. Worrying about Josh is enough to handle right now."

"Then it's the least I can do." She hung up and faced Naomi. "Up for a road trip?"

"To return the brooch?"

Liz nodded. "Renee wants it to go back to the family."

"They didn't leave very long before Renee and Mary Ann. I imagine the Conrads should be home by now."

"Think I should call first?"

"Probably. After today's events, they might assume we're nosy neighbors instead of friends."

Liz went straight to her quarters, found her contact list for the wedding, and placed the call. "Huh. No answer."

"Where else would they be?"

"Maybe they don't want to speak to anyone." Liz hung up. "I hate to bother them, but Renee really wants the brooch back in their possession."

"Let's take our chances and drive over."

After donning jackets and collecting purses, they were soon seated in Liz's Acura. The autumn sun had dipped, the temperature had dropped, and shadows wisped by as she drove.

Liz headed north toward the Conrads' sprawling home, located outside of town. Leaves had begun falling from the trees, and the rich reds, bright oranges, and deep browns created a beautiful color palette. Liz enjoyed this time of year. The corn harvest was nearly upon them, which would leave the fields brown and vacant until spring when planting started again.

"I love the changing leaves," Naomi said, "but once the fields are empty, it's kind of depressing."

"I never really understood harvesttime when I lived in the city. Since coming to Pleasant Creek, I have a whole new appreciation for farmers and their crops."

"Weren't you going to plant a vegetable garden this summer?"

"Yes. Kiera and I had many ideas to spruce up the grounds, but we didn't get around to all of them. Maybe next spring."

"If I wasn't so busy—Liz, slow down!"

Liz eased her foot from the accelerator and glanced at Naomi.

"Is it my imagination, or are there flashing red lights coming from the cornfield up ahead?"

Liz looked down the road, and she also spotted the lights. Drawing closer, she pulled off the road and parked. "Hey, there's a car in there."

In their high heels, the women trudged through the loose soil and around broken cornstalks to get to the stranded vehicle.

"Is anyone inside?" Naomi asked as she veered to the passenger side.

"I hear voices." Just as Liz got to the driver's side door, it opened.

Light spilled from the interior, illuminating the judge. Liz peered inside. Mrs. Conrad was speaking on her cell phone.

The judge crawled out from behind the wheel.

Liz moved out of his way, alarmed by his dazed expression. "Are you okay?"

"Shook up."

She noticed a gash on his forehead and blood trickling down the side of his face. She pointed. "You're hurt."

"What?" The judge ran a shaky hand over his head. When he saw blood on his fingers, his face turned ashen. He took a handkerchief from his pocket and pressed it against the cut.

"Other than your head, are either of you hurt?"

"We were rattled around a bit, but I think we're fine."

"What happened?"

"I don't want to upset Elyse." He glanced at the car, then drew Liz a few feet away. "My brakes went out."

Liz gasped.

"When I realized they weren't working, I steered into the field. The cornstalks slowed down the car. Eventually it stopped."

A siren sounded in the distance.

"I should check on Elyse," the judge said.

"I'll wave down the police." Plodding back to the road, Liz reached the shoulder as the patrol car slowed down.

Officer Dixon parked and joined Liz. "What happened?"

"We were driving to the Conrads' house and noticed a car in the field. The judge and his wife were inside."

"Hurt?"

"The judge has a cut on his forehead. He's bleeding."

They arrived at the scene as Mrs. Conrad staggered out of the car. The judge and Naomi caught her and held her up.

When the officer started asking questions, the judge raised a hand. "Can the ladies take my wife to their car?"

"Certainly."

By the time they had Mrs. Conrad settled in the backseat of Liz's sedan, the woman's teeth chattered uncontrollably. Liz started the car and turned on the heat, then draped a blanket over Mrs. Conrad's shoulders. Naomi sat beside her, murmuring words of comfort, while Liz slid behind the wheel.

Minutes later, Chief Houghton pulled up alongside Liz's car and got out. "Everyone okay here?"

Liz rolled down her window. "Naomi and I are fine. The judge and his wife, on the other hand, had quite a wild ride."

"And you happened by because . . . ?"

"We were driving to their house to return a piece of jewelry for Renee."

The chief looked over the top of her car at the scene. "How did you find them in the field?"

"The hazard lights were flashing. That's how Naomi noticed the car."

He poked his head in the open window. "Mrs. Conrad."

"Chief." Her voice shook. "Please check on my husband."

The chief eyed Liz. "Stay with her until I get back."

Liz nodded.

After the chief left, Mrs. Conrad said, "Thanks for stopping."

"Of course," Naomi told her. "We were actually driving to your house."

"You have news about Josh?"

"No." Naomi patted her hand. "Renee wanted us to return the brooch to you."

Liz removed it from her coat pocket and handed it to Mrs. Conrad. She stared at it for a mere moment, then burst into tears. Naomi put her arm around the hysterical mother.

Liz jumped out of the car when the chief returned.

"The judge insists he's okay," the chief told her. "I'm going to drive him home. In light of Mrs. Conrad's state, I don't want to disturb her, so will you follow me to their house?"

"Yes." She reached out to stop him, her fingers curling around the fabric of his jacket. "Do you think the judge was right? Did his brakes give out?"

The chief gave her a suspicious look.

Liz had been on the receiving end of his reservations before and needed to explain. "He mentioned it when we arrived."

The chief nodded, apparently assured by her answer. "There's no way to know until we have the vehicle inspected."

"And if it was deliberate?"

"Then I have two investigations on my hands."

5

"The two events must be related," Sadie announced the next afternoon.

She and Mary Ann had opened Sew Welcome for a few hours on Sunday for the after-church crowd. Once the breakfast guests had dispersed, Liz joined her friends and Renee, who still appeared shell-shocked. They were discussing the current state of events.

"I'm sure the judge has made a few enemies over the years," Liz said, sipping coffee. The women had opted for hot beverages this afternoon. The day had dawned bright, but the temperature had dipped low enough to form a light coating of frost on the grass and the chill had never left the air.

"Even if the judge has enemies, what does that have to do with Josh?" Renee reasoned. "He works at the bank."

"What better way to make a point to the judge than to hurt him through his family?"

Mary Ann elbowed Sadie. "It might be a coincidence."

"At least no one was badly hurt," Liz said. "I've had quite a few calls from folks wanting to know what they can do to help."

Liz had learned that Pleasant Creek residents rallied around one another in times of need. Between Josh's disappearance and the judge's faulty brakes, this qualified as one of those occasions.

Right now, though, Liz wanted Renee to focus on Josh and the bank. "Any more insight into Josh's job?"

"I thought back to our conversations. He talked about a new business and the possibility of writing a big loan. I was so focused on the wedding plans that I didn't pay much attention." Renee drew in a deep breath. "Here he was, trying to include me in his work life like I asked, and I totally ignored him."

"Josh told me he didn't understand the whole wedding-fever thing, but I'm sure he appreciated that you had things well in hand," Liz assured her. "Don't fret over it."

Renee dabbed at her eyes with a tissue. "It's so easy to think about what I could have done or said differently. Now every conversation we had seems like a missed opportunity."

"What else can you tell us about this new business?" Liz probed. "A name?"

"Josh didn't mention a name. He was concerned because he was having problems with the loan. Again, instead of listening I was going over lists in my head."

"Don't beat yourself up over it," Sadie said.

"Easier said than done," Renee replied.

"Tomorrow I'll stop by the bank," Liz said. "Maybe one of the staff can answer a few questions."

"Mr. Fairfield is the manager," Renee said. "Ask for him."

Conversation wound down after that. Renee went to the kitchen to refill her coffee.

Mary Ann suggested they close the shop since there were no customers. "I'll take Renee home and see if I can get her to eat."

"I'll come with you," Sadie offered. "I can convince anyone to do what I want if I keep talking."

Liz held back a chuckle. Sadie did have a way of making people do things.

"How about you, Liz?"

"I'm headed out to Miriam's. She told me Grace had created her own quilt design, so I gathered some fabric remnants. She's such a sweetheart, and I want to surprise her."

Miriam Borkholder was Liz's second cousin, and they had become close. Grace and Keturah, Miriam's youngest children, had been drawn to Liz from the first time they met.

The Borkholders had embraced Liz once they learned she was

family, even though Liz didn't practice the Amish lifestyle. They were her only family since her mother had passed, leaving Liz a legacy of finding her roots.

"Along with getting catch-up time with Miriam?"

"Every chance I get."

"Miriam has been a great addition as a quilt instructor," Sadie said. "Since we've scheduled classes with her, more of our visiting quilters are asking for her."

"She's talented. Who wouldn't want her as a teacher?"

It was a short drive to Miriam's big, white house. As Liz navigated the gravel driveway, she noticed a few horse-drawn wagons parked near the barn. Children frolicked in the yard. A group of men dressed in dark pants, blue shirts, and wide-brimmed hats gathered around a project. She spotted Miriam's husband, Philip, their son Isaac, and, if she wasn't mistaken, Caleb Hoffner. She'd met Caleb only once at Miriam's house because Josh happened to be with him. Now Liz wanted to find out exactly what Caleb knew. The only problem? She doubted the young man would speak to her, especially with others from the community nearby.

Miriam rose from her rocking chair on the porch, setting aside her sewing to meet Liz. "*Hallo.* I am so happy to see you."

"Likewise," Liz said as she hugged her cousin. "I have a gift for Grace. I hope this isn't a bad time."

"*Nay.* Philip is busy, and I am mending the girls' dresses. Come. Tell me what you have brought."

"When you told me about Grace's quilt design, I couldn't resist gathering some fabric. Do you think she'll like it?"

"Oh my. How generous. Grace will be very grateful."

"The design is quite complicated, especially for a twelve-year-old. I was hoping I could display the quilt at the inn once she is finished. Is that okay with you?"

"Yes, and I am sure she will be honored." Miriam gazed at the children, her pretty features turning soft. "She is such a good girl."

"I'll set the bag here." Liz plopped down on a rocker. "I could use a few minutes of peace."

Miriam sat down too. "I heard about Renee's wedding. I am sorry it did not take place."

"Poor Renee is a mess. Josh is still missing. No one knows what to think."

"So you allow *Gött* to take care of the situation."

"Believe me, I have sent up more than one prayer since Josh went missing."

Miriam resumed her sewing. "Have faith."

"I will. Especially for Renee's sake."

"Chief Houghton made inquiries here. Even if anyone saw Josh, we would not say anything to the police." She sighed. "But I do wish we could help."

As Liz had learned in the past, the Amish were reluctant to get involved in affairs of the English.

A shout went up from the children.

Liz smiled. "What's new around here? Sarah hasn't had much to tell me lately."

"Sarah is busy taking care of my son, so she has not been around the house. Married life is treating them well."

"Good to hear. You know I have a special place in my heart for Sarah. She's an amazing employee."

"Actually, Isaac is here today, helping his father."

"I'm sure Philip appreciates it."

Miriam set the fabric in her lap. "I don't believe you know the other men, although Caleb Hoffner is here."

"I suppose he heard about the wedding."

"Yes. I imagine he is quite concerned."

"Do you think he might speak to me?" Liz knew it was a long shot, but she had to give it a try.

Miriam hesitated before answering. "I do not think so." She stood. "Grace, come here."

Grace ran over, skipping up the porch steps. When she noticed Liz, she smiled.

"I'm so glad to see you," Liz said. "I have something for you."

Grace looked at her mother, then at Liz. "What is it?"

Liz handed Grace the bag of fabric. "Your mother told me about your quilt design. I was wondering if you'd make the quilt out of this fabric. Then I'd like to display it at the inn."

"Truly?"

"Yes."

Grace gently pulled back the edges of the bag, her gray eyes wide. "It is okay, *Mutter*?"

Miriam took her seat. "Because it is from Liz, yes, it is fine."

With her mother's permission, Grace dug into the bag. Her smile warmed Liz's heart. After studying the remnants, she replaced them neatly in the bag. When another child called her name, Grace raced down the steps and disappeared around the side of the house.

"I think the fabric is a hit," Liz said with a satisfied smile.

"I agree."

Liz and Miriam visited for a while, catching up on life.

Isaac rounded the house carrying a bucket filled with rags. He met Liz's gaze. "Cousin, it is good to see you."

"Likewise. You must have a big project going on back there."

"A broken axle on the wagon."

"You are finished?" Miriam asked.

"Yes. Thank you, *Mutter*." He held up the bucket. "I will bring this inside before going home."

Just then a wagon plodded by, followed by another with children in the back and still another carrying a few more men.

"Looks like everyone is leaving," Liz observed. Did that mean Caleb was going back to his farm? She had come to see Grace, but she hoped to have an opportunity to question Caleb since he was here.

"It is nearly time for the evening meal." Miriam rose. "Which I must prepare."

Liz stood. "I should get back to the inn. Most of the guests left after the wedding was canceled, but a few relatives stayed. I need to set out the afternoon snack and make coffee."

"*Dänka*, Liz. For the visit and Grace's gift."

"My pleasure. I'll see you at your next class." Liz started her car and waved good-bye. As always, she enjoyed her time at Miriam's. She drove down the driveway with every intention of turning toward town, but instead she headed in the opposite direction. She hadn't glimpsed Caleb in any of the wagons that were leaving. What were the odds he was walking home? Here in Amish country, very good odds indeed.

Almost half a mile up the road, she spotted a young man walking along the edge of the field. She passed and glanced in her rearview mirror. As luck would have it, Caleb lumbered right in her direction.

Liz pulled over, turned off the ignition, and stepped out of the car. "Caleb, a minute?"

The young man froze. He glanced down the road, as if deciding if he should run. He muttered under his breath and approached her.

"I'm glad I saw you. I wanted to ask you about Josh."

"I do not know anything. I told the police chief as well," he said a bit testily. He looked at the ground, the field, and the sky, never meeting Liz's gaze. She'd questioned enough witnesses to know when a person was hiding something.

"I figured since you two are friends, he must have visited you before the wedding."

"Please don't ask me."

"Please don't lie."

His eyes met hers. "Why would you say that?"

"Because you're nervous. You know something."

Caleb shuffled, shoving his hands deep into his pockets. "I promised."

"Josh?"

Caleb nodded.

"Promised him what?"

"That I wouldn't tell anyone he came here yesterday morning." Caleb took his hat off and ruffled his shaggy blond hair. "I know I am not to say a word, but I am worried."

Sensing an opening, Liz spoke gently. "I don't think your community would mind if you helped a friend."

Caleb seemed to consider her words, even though his struggle was clear. He finally said, "Josh was under stress. The wedding was too much, his job had him worried, and he and his father had argued again. He came to sit with me by the pond so we could talk."

"Josh and his dad argued? About what?"

"Judge Conrad never liked that Josh majored in finance. He wanted Josh to be a lawyer like him. Now that Josh was getting married, his father wanted him to return to school and get a law degree. He did not think much of Josh's job at the bank."

"What did Josh want?"

"He likes his job. He finally told his father he wasn't going back to school. They had words."

"Do you think Josh wanted to leave town? Leave Renee?"

"No. He might be mad at his father, but he would never leave Renee. He loves her."

"Why didn't he come to the inn?"

"I do not know. He said he was going to live his life no matter what his father thought. The last I saw him he was driving toward town." Caleb put his hat back on. "When his friend came here looking for him, I knew there was some kind of trouble."

"I appreciate you telling me."

"You see why I could not tell the chief? This is a family matter."

"And I'll keep it that way."

A few silent moments passed, and neither of them moved.

Then Caleb spoke. "I do not think he ran."

"I don't think so either."

A crow flew overhead, sweeping low. The deep scent of harvest soil lingered in the cool air. A chill crept up Liz's spine. Where had Josh gone after seeing Caleb? Did anyone else know that he and his father had had a disagreement?

"Josh did not want Renee to know what was going on with his father. And he especially did not want her to know he had problems at work. He said he did not want to burden her with the steps he had to take."

"What steps?"

"I do not know. But it was something to do with the bank."

"I'll check into it. If for some reason Josh returns, please convince him to talk to Renee. She's worried sick."

"One more thing," Caleb said. "Josh usually turns his phone off when he visits, but he must have forgotten. Just before he left, someone called him. His face turned red, but he didn't answer. When he got in his car, I watched him press buttons on his phone, like maybe he was seeing who had called. Then he drove away."

"Thank you. I won't tell anyone we spoke." Liz turned to leave, then stopped. "Why didn't you come to the wedding?"

His face turned red. "I had work on the farm and could not get away. I felt bad because I never told Josh I could not attend."

"He would have understood."

"Yes. Josh is a good *Freund.*" Caleb walked away.

So Josh had received a call. Had he planned another stop before the wedding? Since no one had heard from him, she couldn't know for sure. But Liz remembered his tone the night he'd been pacing the four-season room. If the caller was the same person Josh spoke to that night, there was plenty of animosity between them.

On the drive back to the inn, Liz got a headache from trying to piece together all the events. Nothing made sense. Yes, Josh was stressed. Who wasn't before a wedding? But pile on the suggestions that there was trouble at work and the argument with his father the morning of the wedding, and things became even worse. What else could go wrong?

But the phone calls troubled Liz the most. Evidently, Josh had problems he didn't want to share with anyone. They still didn't know if he'd taken off or if something had happened to him. She'd try to get answers at the bank tomorrow.

As she drove past a cornfield, her heart sank. Could Josh's car be stuck in a field somewhere too? Could he be hurt and no one the wiser? A victim of foul play? She said a silent prayer for Josh's safety.

Instead of the situation becoming clearer the more she learned, the facts only grew more muddled.

6

The next morning sped by as Liz fed the last of the inn guests, checked them out after a disappointing end to the wedding weekend, and gave Sarah a list of tasks to complete while Liz was gone. Satisfied things were well in hand, she put on a navy suit from her attorney days and prepared to speak to the manager at Pleasant Creek Savings and Loan.

Twenty minutes later she arrived at the bank and held the door open for an elderly woman with a cane.

"Thank you, my dear."

"My pleasure." Liz watched the woman slowly make her way to the teller window.

Liz approached the receptionist's desk, manned by a fifty-something woman with her graying hair pulled into a severe bun and a look on her face that said she regularly suffered from heartburn. She wasn't the cheerful receptionist Liz was used to seeing at the bank. "Good morning. I'd like to speak to Mr. Fairfield."

"Do you have an appointment?"

"No. I was hoping he might have a few minutes."

"He's a very busy man."

"I do my banking here, and I was told if I ever need *anything*, all I had to do was ask. There shouldn't be a problem speaking to the man in charge, right?"

The woman considered Liz's words before picking up her phone. She pressed a button and waited. "Sir? A customer would like to see you." When she hung up, she pointed to a grouping of chairs and a sideboard with a coffeemaker. "Please have a seat."

"Thanks."

Before Liz made it to the sitting area, a loud voice stopped her. "Is there a problem, Ms. Eckardt?"

Liz turned to see a reed-thin man with a receding hairline and thick glasses walking toward her, his boisterous tone at odds with his slight body. "You remember me?" She'd met Mr. Fairfield only once when she set up her bank account after purchasing the inn.

"I know all my customers. Let's go to my office."

Once there, she realized he'd seen her come in because his desk was strategically placed in front of a large window, providing a view of the lobby.

"Please sit. What can I do for you today?"

She explained about Josh missing his own wedding.

"I am aware of the situation. Chief Houghton asked me questions, but he has the authority to do so."

Point taken. Liz knew she couldn't force the issue legally. She'd never expected to, but she'd hoped the manager would give her a general idea of the work situation out of concern for his employee. "In light of Josh missing his wedding, I'm wondering if you can provide some insight on any problems he might have been experiencing at work that would have kept him away."

Mr. Fairfield frowned. "This is highly irregular."

"I agree."

"I can't give you any information about our employees."

"That's not what I'm asking." Liz scooted to the edge of her seat. "Josh isn't the type to disappear without a word."

"Yes, it's true. Josh is a very responsible person."

"So I understand. Renee is devastated, and she asked me to check into the matter for her. She mentioned something about a loan Josh was working on."

"Josh works on many loans. That's the nature of his job."

"Right. We were curious if anything unusual had happened to him lately. Perhaps an encounter with an unhappy customer."

"He comes to work, sees customers, does paperwork, and goes home. Beyond that information, I'm afraid I'm not at liberty to say."

Just as she thought, but she'd needed to try anyway. She stood and said, "Thank you."

Mr. Fairfield rose. "Is there anything related to your account that I can help you with?"

"Not today." Liz left the office and returned to the lobby. When she reached the door, she saw the same elderly lady she'd let in earlier. Together they walked out to the sidewalk.

The woman tapped her cane on the concrete. "You won't get any help from the bank folks. They're tighter than Fort Knox."

"Excuse me?"

"I've seen that same look on Fairfield's face when he won't do something a customer requests. Are fresh cookies really too much to ask for?"

"I don't think so."

"I pay service fees. I should have nice treats and freshly brewed coffee when I come in for business. Food is as bad here as at the center," the woman declared.

Liz grinned, already liking this woman. "I'm Liz Eckardt."

"Betty Hulbert."

"Nice to meet you."

Betty narrowed her eyes. "Josh's wedding was supposed to be at your inn."

"You heard about what happened?"

"The non-wedding, you mean?"

Liz tried not to grimace. In a town as small as Pleasant Creek, it didn't take much for bad news—or any news, for that matter—to spread quickly. "Yes. How do you know Josh?"

"Every time I visit the bank he comes out of his office to greet me. That's the kind of nice young man he is."

Not the type of man to stand up his bride at the altar.

"I imagine sweet Renee is a basket case," Betty continued.
"You know her?"

"Josh has mentioned her."

"Right," Liz said. "We're hoping he turns up soon."

"He will."

"How can you be so sure?"

"I've lived a long life. In my experience, things always work out for the best."

"For Renee's sake, I hope so."

Betty tapped her cane again. "Let me get to the point. I couldn't help but hear your conversation with Fairfield."

"How on earth?"

"He left his door open, and I happened to be standing nearby. People always assume that because one is elderly, one can't hear. I have perfect hearing. Good sight. And my own teeth."

Liz found her gaze momentarily drawn to the woman's teeth. "Um, good to know."

"And I know Josh had a very disgruntled customer in here last week."

"Because you happened to overhear his conversation too?"

"Dear, the entire bank heard it. Pete Hardy yelled at Josh, saying Josh couldn't repossess his truck for a few missed payments because it would take away his livelihood. If the bank took his livelihood, he couldn't pay off the loan. You know the story. Then a young man came in asking to change the day his payment is withdrawn from his account because he'd landed a new job and his payday was different." Betty shook her head. "Josh is always putting out one fire or another."

"I don't see how—"

"Let me finish."

Liz pressed her lips together.

"Josh took the young man into his office to discuss the problem. Pete, on the other hand, stood right in the lobby going on and on about permits, the government making his life miserable, and how it wasn't his fault the world was conspiring against him. Fairfield finally made him leave."

"The world? Isn't that a little much?"

"Typical hothead, but you didn't hear that from me." Betty crossed her arms. "For now, the taco truck's future is in limbo."

"Taco truck?"

"Pete's business. Tacos on Tires. We love his food, so he's a regular at the senior center. Well, he was."

Repossessed trucks and hotheads were entertaining but not the information Liz needed. Pete sounded more like a man making excuses for not paying his debt than a person who would actually follow through on his threats.

"Any other tidbits you've picked up while visiting the bank?"

"No. That's the latest hubbub." A car horn sounded down the street. "That's my ride."

"Betty, it's been a pleasure."

"Likewise, Liz." She flashed a smile so big and bright that Liz couldn't help but notice her natural teeth again. "I've heard about your breakfast at the inn. Sometime I'd like to check it out."

"Usually breakfast is reserved for my guests, but you sound like a real cookie connoisseur. I'll invite you over to taste my baking."

"Have anything as good as Mary Ann's pies?"

"Her pies are in a class of their own, but I think my baking will pass your critique."

"It's a date."

The horn sounded again.

Betty turned and shook her cane at the driver. "Hold your horses. I'm coming."

Liz made sure the woman reached the car, then headed back to the inn, not entirely sure if her trip had garnered any results.

She went straight to Sew Welcome. "The bank was a bust," she announced as she entered. "Not that I expected much."

"Those bank charges will get you every time," Sadie said unnaturally loud.

Liz realized why when she caught sight of Judge and Mrs. Conrad sitting with Sadie and Mary Ann on the chairs used during quilting classes.

"The Conrads stopped by to see if there were any loose ends to take care of regarding the wedding."

"After all you've been through," Liz said as she crossed the room, "you don't need to worry."

Mrs. Conrad, eyes red, grasped a tissue. "We can't sit around and wait. We have to do something."

"Elyse," the judge said, squeezing her other hand, "the authorities are handling the search."

Liz met Sadie's gaze. "Has the chief made it official?"

"We haven't heard, but I have faith they'll find Josh."

"I hope," Mrs. Conrad said before she burst out crying.

Liz noticed the judge grimace and decided to give him a little breathing room. "Judge, why don't you come with me while I get coffee for everyone?"

His hasty move to stand told Liz he'd been listening to his wife's crying for a long time.

They went to the kitchen where Liz scooped coffee into a filter, added water, and started the maker.

"It's been a tough couple of days," the judge said, leaning against the counter.

"I can't even begin to imagine. Josh missing, your car going off the road." She glanced at the cut on his forehead. A bluish bruise surrounded it. "Are you doing okay?"

"My head will heal," he said. "But my heart won't until we know Josh is safe and sound."

Liz didn't know what to say. She'd never had children, but she'd raised her godson, Steve, after his parents died in a car crash when he was seven. Now he was in the military and stationed in Kosovo, and she worried about him. She used an online video chat service to speak to him frequently and knew he was okay. But if he ever went missing, she'd be as much of a wreck as Mrs. Conrad.

The coffee finished brewing. Liz poured the judge a big mug because he looked like he could use it, then filled cups for the ladies. "I'll take these to the store. Are you joining us?"

He shook his head. "Do you mind if I spend a few minutes in the four-season room? I have some calls to make."

"Take your time." Liz placed the coffee cups on a tray along with cream and sugar and went back to serve the ladies.

A few customers had stopped in. Mary Ann waited on them while Sadie sat with Mrs. Conrad, still in serious conversation.

"Here you go," Liz said, setting the tray on a small table far away from the shelves of fabric.

Mrs. Conrad took a cup, her hands shaking, and continued talking as if Liz hadn't just joined them. "Josh is kind to everyone. I can't imagine anyone wanting to hurt him. Or that he'd run away. He loves Renee."

"It does seem odd," Sadie agreed.

"It must have to do with one of my husband's cases," she went on. "That's the only explanation. His decisions aren't always popular."

At Mrs. Conrad's words, a lightbulb went on in Liz's head. Could Josh have been kidnapped in retaliation for a ruling made by the judge?

"I'll be right back," she told Sadie, then rushed to the other side of the inn. She found the judge staring out the back window at the spot where his son should have been married. "Judge, a minute?"

He turned and held up his mug. "Great coffee."

"Thanks. I was thinking, could a court case you've worked on in the past somehow be connected to Josh's disappearance?"

The judge heaved out a long sigh. "That very idea has kept me awake for two nights now."

"And?"

"I rarely deal with violent criminals."

"What do you deal with?"

"Municipal affairs. Civil issues."

Not exactly situations that would cause a person to stoop to kidnapping. "So nothing?"

"Oh, there is something." He set his mug on the side table and lowered himself onto the couch. Liz joined him. "I was right. According to Chief Houghton, the brake lines on my car were cut."

Liz gaped.

"I've gone over past cases, but nothing I've ruled on seems to be serious enough for someone to want to harm me or my family." Judge Conrad ran a hand over his forehead and winced when he touched the cut. "I have my clerk studying cases to see if I'm wrong."

"I know legal rulings aren't always popular."

"You were an attorney, correct?"

"In my previous life, yes. As I remember, the losing party is never happy."

"Unhappy I could take. But losing my son because of a legal decision? Torture."

"I hope your clerk finds something to go on."

"I don't expect much. I mostly handle speeding tickets, permit problems, safety codes—cases like that."

Liz remembered what Helen had told her at the bank. "Like permits for food trucks?"

"Yes. Tacos on Tires has been especially trying."

"Sounds like the owner has problems."

"Pete Hardy parks where he shouldn't, doesn't pay his fines, and complains when he ends up before me. If he spent as much time attending to his business as he does fighting tickets, he'd be a rich man."

"So he is a problem?"

He met her gaze head-on. "If you think Pete could have anything to do with Josh's disappearance, think again. He's a complainer, not a man of action."

The judge has already considered Pete. Good.

But hearing Pete's name twice in one day had Liz's antenna up. The fact that Pete had yelled at Josh at the bank raised red flags. The judge might brush off Pete, but until she spoke to the man in question, she wouldn't count him out as a suspect. She wouldn't worry the judge about her hunch until she had concrete information. There was no point in keeping the man up at night any more than he already was.

"I understand you and Josh had words before the wedding."

The judge flinched. "How . . . ?"

"Josh confided in a friend, who told me."

"I'm not proud of it, but we had an ongoing disagreement about his career. I felt I had one last chance to state my case about him attending law school." He hung his head. "We argued. The last words we spoke to each other were angry and cruel."

"I'm sorry."

"I love my son and thought I knew better when telling him how to live his life. Now I'd give anything to apologize and I can't." The pain reflected in the judge's eyes tore at her heart. "It's been killing me to think I might be the reason he left."

"He'll be found."

"I'll never bring up law school to him again. He's happy in finance. I stubbornly refused to accept his love for numbers."

It wasn't a great way to reconcile your child's profession, but the judge seemed sincere. For his sake, Liz hoped he wasn't the reason Josh left. She could only pray the judge got a chance to tell Josh that he'd changed his mind concerning his career choice.

7

The next morning, after serving a hearty breakfast to her only guests, two sisters from Michigan who were in town to shop at Sew Welcome, Liz called Judge Conrad's clerk. He'd checked the cases the judge had presided over, compiling a list of potential persons of interest, but he would only give the list to the police chief. *So much for remaining in the loop.*

Since the inn had been booked solid for the wedding and the next few days were slow, Liz and Sarah were scheduled to thoroughly clean the guest rooms. Armed with supplies, she joined the young woman upstairs.

"Which room would you like to start in?" Sarah asked, donning an apron over her gray dress.

"How about I take the third-floor rooms? You can start with the Somewhere in Time Room."

Sarah grabbed her supply bin and got busy with her assignment.

Liz climbed the stairs to the Sunrise and Sunset Rooms. Both were single occupancy with a shared bathroom. The clean, contemporary decor included white walls, baskets, and colorful wall art and cushions. She'd carried the bright theme into the bathroom, which she tackled first. Then she moved on to vacuuming, dusting, and general fussing.

When Liz finished, she pressed her palm to the small of her back as she stretched the kinks out. She gazed out the window and grinned. The lovely day gifted them with beautiful blue skies and sunshine bright enough to put anyone in a good mood. The vantage point from the third floor provided a clear view of downtown Pleasant Creek, and she noticed a large, yellow van parked in front of town hall. She squinted. *Tacos on Tires* blazed in bold red letters. How on earth had she never seen it?

At the thought of tacos, her stomach rumbled. Maybe now would be a good time to meet the truck vendor. She had a few questions for him.

She trotted down the stairs and found Sarah. "Have you seen the taco truck around town?"

"It is rather hard to miss."

Liz put her hands on her hips. "Where have I been? I just heard about it."

"I cannot say. But the truck has been around for a while."

"Hmm. And is the food any good?"

"I have never eaten it."

"Because it's not Amish?"

A sly grin passed over Sarah's lips. "No, because I don't like spicy food."

Liz laughed. "There you go." She glanced at her watch. "I'm hungry, so I'm going over there for lunch. Take a break and then finish up. I'll get to the pumpkin muffins later this afternoon. The Smith sisters are leaving tomorrow and hinted they'd like something with fall flair for breakfast."

"Do not tell Miss Mason, but your pumpkin and cranberry muffins are especially good."

"Naomi won't mind, but let's keep that our little secret."

Sarah went to the kitchen, and Liz dashed off to her quarters to change into a pullover and jeans before walking to the taco truck.

Soon she stood in line, waiting behind folks who obviously had fallen victim to the lure of Tacos on Tires.

"Come here often?" sounded a male voice behind her.

She turned and smiled at Jackson Cross, the mayor. "No, I just heard about the food truck. Don't tell me you're here for lunch as well."

"Afraid I am. Pete makes a mean taco."

"Is there such a thing?"

"Give me your answer after you've tasted one."

"Where has this guy been hiding out?" Liz asked.

"He normally parks in specific places, like north of Main on Mondays, the senior center on Wednesdays, and out by the interstate the rest of the week. This is the first time in months he's parked here."

"Permit problems?"

He raised his eyebrows. "And you know this how?"

"Judge Conrad. It kind of came up in conversation."

Jackson laughed. "You probably know more than I do. I don't see Pete much."

"Pete's been selling tacos for a long time?"

"On and off. He has a tendency to . . . get over his head in business."

"Next," a voice growled.

Jackson motioned to the truck. "I believe it's your turn to order."

"Right." Liz turned and faced the menu board mounted on the wall. "Two chicken tacos with the works and a side of chips and salsa."

"Wow," Jackson said. "Hungry?"

Liz glanced over her shoulder. "Starving. It's cleaning day at the inn."

She studied Pete as he filled her order. Fortyish, she guessed, by the look of his dull, slightly graying hair and the lines around his eyes. He was a bit overweight, his stomach straining at his worn T-shirt. Pete moved with an economy of motion, knowing exactly where to locate the ingredients for the dish he prepared. He placed her order in a bag, set it on the counter, and told Liz how much she owed.

Liz paid him, then took the bag.

"Hey, if you don't mind waiting we can eat lunch together," Jackson suggested.

"Sure." Liz always enjoyed the mayor's company, along with his genuine smile and rugged good looks. And because he was a fellow businessperson, she liked to bounce ideas off him once in a while. He was very different from the urbane men she'd worked with in Boston. She hadn't thought she'd ever be attracted to the outdoorsy type, but her opinion changed after she'd met Jackson. Not that they'd talked about seeing each other socially or if she was even in the market to date.

After Jackson picked up his order, they walked to the steps of the town hall and sat down.

"Once this weather changes, it'll be a while before we're eating lunch outside again."

"True." Liz took a bite of her taco and closed her eyes. A myriad of flavors danced on her tongue. The tender, seasoned meat and the salsa tasted of perfection. She opened her eyes and stared at Jackson. "This is the best taco I've ever eaten. I ran into an older lady yesterday, and she mentioned how much the seniors love his food. Now I get it."

"Pete knows his way around spicy food."

"I still can't believe I didn't know about him. What were you saying about Pete getting over his head in business?"

"He has a habit of getting into trouble from time to time. He might be a genius when it comes to tacos, but most of the decisions he makes in life? Not so much."

"What do you mean?"

"He's worked in kitchens from here to Chicago and back but could never hold a job."

"Why not?"

"Anger issues, for one. He got arrested a few years ago and thinks everyone is out to get him."

"Are they?"

"No. Pete's his own worst enemy. Has been as long as I've known him, and we go back to high school."

"He seems to have found his calling."

"After an uncle died and left him some money, he bought the truck, started his concept, and hit the road. Until the money ran out and he came home."

"Ah. That explains the bank loan."

"Too bad he can't get his act together. He has a good business going." Jackson took a bite of his taco.

"That's high praise coming from a man who knows the ropes of running a successful business." Liz smiled. Jackson was not only the mayor of Pleasant Creek but the owner of Cross Furniture.

"What can I say? My dad was a great teacher, and I happen to enjoy the family business. But furniture and food are vastly different. Besides, I don't think Pete would ever take any advice."

"Too bad. You could give him some solid business pointers."

"He's not an accepting kind of guy."

She polished off her taco. "His food is incredible."

"And he wins a lot of competitions."

"Even with his short fuse?"

"Yep." Jackson finished his food and tossed the wrapper in the empty bag. He rose. "Before I go, tell me how Renee is doing."

"Destroyed, as you can imagine. She's staying with Mary Ann. The Material Girls are pitching in any way we can."

He glanced at the taco truck. "By figuring out the connection between Josh and Pete's bank loan?"

"Anyone ever told you you're one smart guy?"

Jackson winked at her. "All I can say is good luck with that plan."

Liz watched him walk inside town hall, then cleaned up after her lunch. By the time she finished, Pete stepped out of the truck with a big bag of trash.

Liz approached him. "Excuse me, Pete?"

He stopped, narrowing his eyes. "Yeah."

"I'm Liz Eckardt. Owner of the Olde Mansion Inn."

"Competition?"

"Oh, not really. Your food is amazing."

He seemed to relax. "Thanks."

"I was wondering if you knew about Josh Conrad."

"The dude's always out to get me."

"Pardon?"

"He and the bank make my life miserable." Pete looked disgusted.

"I'm sorry, but that's not what I meant. Josh is missing."

His expression didn't change. "So?"

"You were heard threatening him at the bank last week."

"Because he wanted to take my truck."

"And now he's missing."

Realization flashed across Pete's face. "You gotta be kidding me. You think I did something to Josh?"

"I'm only asking if you know where he might be."

"News flash, lady. Me and Josh might get into it over money, but I'd never hurt him. Besides, I've been trying to get my payment and permit problems straightened out before a big food-truck competition out of town. I don't have time for Josh."

"What about his father?"

"I got no use for the judge." Pete stomped away, muttering.

"Your food is really good," Liz called out. "Good luck."

She thought Pete seemed too distracted by his own issues to have anything to do with Josh's disappearance. But by his own admission, he and Josh had had run-ins over his loan. Could he have gone over the edge? Done something to Josh to keep him from repossessing the taco truck before the competition?

Pete slung the trash bag into a trash receptacle in the alley, then trudged back. "You still here?"

"Sorry. I didn't mean to imply—"

"Just hit the road. I got stuff to do." He climbed into the truck, slammed the serving window shut, and fired up the engine. Moments later he turned east off Main Street.

"That went well," she said to no one, not entirely sure if Pete knew anything or not.

On impulse, Liz stopped by Sweet Everything on the way to the inn. Sugary-scented air greeted her as she walked in. Naomi had replaced her usual coral color scheme with autumn decorations, featuring bright yellow chrysanthemums in the bud vases on the tables and cutouts of fall leaves around the edges of the large display case.

"Any news on Josh?" Naomi asked from behind the counter.

"Unfortunately, no."

"Where could he be?"

"That's the question of the hour." Liz summarized the events of her day. "I'm afraid I haven't been much help."

"You tried."

"I'm not sure what Renee wants us to do. I have no idea how to find Josh."

"Maybe she just wants to know someone is doing something. It has to be torture waiting for word."

"I suppose." Liz had never been good at sitting around waiting for news. If there was a problem to be solved, she always came up with answers. But finding Josh? She ran an inn, for goodness sake, not a private detective agency. Yes, she'd had success solving mysteries in Pleasant Creek in the past, but she didn't make a habit of it. So why was she questioning her skills now?

It was because of Renee's devastated face when she'd learned Josh was missing. The hurt and confusion in her eyes had touched a spot deep inside Liz. The love Renee felt for Josh and, Liz was convinced, the love that Josh returned, had to be strong enough to get them through this situation. For Renee's sake, Liz would have faith that things would work out. And until they did, she'd continue searching, no matter how inadequate she considered her skills.

"Speaking of Renee," Naomi said as she slid a tray of éclairs into the display case. "Why don't we all go over to Mary Ann's later? We can take dinner. If nothing else, spending time with the Material Girls will get Renee's mind off Josh."

"Sounds great. She mentioned that she needs a project for her kindergarten class, so we could assist her. It'll keep her busy for a little while at least."

"What a wonderful idea. I'll call Mary Ann first to okay it, then call the others to let them in on the dinner plans."

"I need to get back to the inn. I have baking to do for tomorrow, but I'll be free for the night."

"Mind if I ask what's on the menu?" Naomi grinned. "Consider it professional curiosity."

"Muffins."

"Pumpkin, by any chance?"

While Liz decided how to answer, Naomi laughed. "I've heard through the grapevine that your muffins rock. If you weren't such a good friend, I might be jealous."

Liz scanned the display case before her. "I highly doubt it. Your baking talents are off the charts. And I've had to shed a few pounds because of your treats."

"Thanks. I appreciate the compliment."

"You're welcome. Here's hoping your sweets give us a short reprieve from wondering where Josh is." Liz swallowed hard. "And if he's okay."

8

"You didn't have to do all this," Mary Ann told Liz as she and the other Material Girls trooped into her house, arms full of food and drinks. "But I'm glad you did."

Liz stomped the leaves off her shoes and glanced at Renee. Her pale face showed how worried she was about Josh. "How is she holding up?"

"Some minutes hopeful, others full of dread."

"No news from the chief?"

Mary Ann shook her head. "But at least he's been patient with Renee's frequent calls. For that alone he deserves a cherry pie."

"His favorite?"

"He's not choosy."

"Any kind you make is heavenly, so I'm sure he'll be a happy man."

They joined the others in the kitchen. Opal removed a large pan from a carrier while Caitlyn unpacked Naomi's bag of rolls, cookies, and pastries.

"I'm glad we invited ourselves to dinner," Sadie announced, taking glasses from the cabinet to add to the already set table. "Opal's spaghetti is the best."

"Baked spaghetti," Opal corrected.

Sadie danced across the room, balancing the glasses. "It's still good."

Liz sidestepped Sadie, then grabbed two jugs of tea from her tote. She looked over her shoulder to find Renee lingering in the doorway, not mixing with the others. How was the girl getting through the hours of not knowing, worried that Josh might be hurt or worse? Or had he just up and left? The questions alone were mind-boggling.

"Renee, why don't you help me pour?"

With a listless shuffle, Renee picked up a jug and carried it to the table. Everyone took their places.

Sadie cleared her throat. "I think we should have a moment of silence and pray for Josh's safety." She patted Renee's hand. "And patience for you, my dear."

The room went silent. Liz could imagine their prayers linked together, making them stronger.

A clap from Sadie broke the reverie. "Now then, let's dig in."

It didn't take long for food to be dished, rolls to be passed, and conversation to flow.

Renee pushed her food around her plate, but at least she was making an effort and eating a few bites. She definitely needed something to take her mind off Josh.

"So, Renee," Naomi started, "Liz mentioned you need a project for your kindergarten class."

"Hmm? Oh yes. Every Christmas each class does a community project. We always start planning early."

"Do you have a specific idea in mind?"

"I was going to start thinking about it when Josh and I got back from our honeymoon . . ." Her voice trailed off.

"No time like the present to come up with an idea," Sadie said in a no-nonsense tone. "Girls?"

Everyone spoke at once.

Sadie clapped again. "One at a time. Opal?"

"Bake sales always raise money."

"We did that last year," Renee said.

"Talent show?" Naomi offered.

"The older grades usually have that covered."

Caitlyn raised her hand.

Sadie chuckled. "This isn't school."

"It sure feels like it."

"What do you suggest?"

Caitlyn straightened in her seat. "Every year various organizations donate to the different floors at the hospital. I found out the group designated to gift the children's wing had to withdraw." Her face grew more animated. "What if we, the Material Girls, put together small stockings? Then Renee's class can fill them with candy or seasonal treats."

Mary Ann smiled. "What a beautiful idea."

They all turned to Renee.

"What do you think?" Liz prompted

Slight color brushed Renee's cheeks. "I think my kids will love it. The PTA usually coordinates each class activity. Now I can give them an update."

"Maybe we can buy cards," Caitlyn added, "and the children in your class can sign their names."

"And include a gift card for the parents," Naomi suggested. "It can be for the entire family."

"What are you proposing?" Liz asked. "That we cut, sew, and, if we have time, quilt the stockings?"

"Exactly," Caitlyn said with a grin that usually meant mischief. "I even brought samples to choose from, just in case you agreed and want to get started."

"So," Sadie said to the group, "are we in?"

A resounding yes was the reply, even from Renee.

Sadie winked at Caitlyn. "Good job."

"I'm glad the group agreed because I already signed us up."

"Why, Caitlyn, that sounds like something I would do," Sadie declared.

"What can I say? I've learned from the best." Caitlyn grinned again.

Soon the women finished dinner, cleared the table, and washed the dishes. They ended up in the living room studying Caitlyn's sample patterns. Renee sat on the couch, her attention on her phone.

"She's been like this since the wedding," Mary Ann whispered to Liz. "I'm worried about her."

"I wish there was more we could do."

"Short of finding Josh, I don't think there is anything else." Mary Ann took the pattern that was passed to her. "Speaking of helping, any luck?"

"Not really. I spoke to a few people, but I don't have much to go on."

"Where could that young man be?"

The conversation turned to the stocking project. The women agreed on a simple pattern that wouldn't be too time-consuming to sew and embellish. The group estimated the number of stockings they needed to make and decided they had plenty of time to get the job done.

As the discussion moved to fabric choices, a *ping* sounded from Renee's phone. She jumped, then picked it up, tapping the screen, her face alight with expectation. A few seconds later she looked discouraged. "Not Josh."

Mary Ann blew out a breath.

Renee typed an answer and set the phone aside.

"I imagine people want to know how you're doing," Sadie said. "Or think they're being helpful by checking in."

"But really," Naomi continued the thought, "you don't want to talk to anyone."

Renee sighed. "Yes. My friends want to know what's going on. I don't blame them. I'm just . . . tired and worried."

"She's not sleeping well," Mary Ann told the group. "Most people know she's staying here, and they call night and day."

"The helpful folks," Sadie said.

"Oh, I don't mind." Renee folded her hands in her lap. "I get that everyone is concerned."

"She's too nice to turn them away," Mary Ann mumbled under her breath.

"Maybe we can get Sadie to guard the door and take the calls," Liz whispered.

"Now you're talking," Mary Ann responded.

"Talking about what?" Sadie asked, not missing a thing.

"I might have a job for you," Mary Ann told her.

Sadie looked from Mary Ann to Renee and back again. "Say the word."

"We'll talk later."

Sadie nodded.

"My bridesmaids have been great," Renee went on. "They check in every couple of hours. And Josh's mom calls every day. I expect that from my close friends, but people I haven't seen in a while are concerned too."

"Pleasant Creek is such a caring community," Opal said as she flipped through a pattern book Caitlyn had supplied.

"I know. I've been out of high school for years, but even a few of my classmates have called."

"Or stopped by." Disgust colored Mary Ann's tone.

For the first time since Josh had disappeared, Renee laughed. "Gee, I can't imagine who you're talking about."

Liz glanced at Mary Ann. "What are we missing here?"

Mary Ann's gaze remained fixed on Renee. "Certain folks are out of your life for a reason."

Caitlyn scooted forward in her seat. "Oh, this must be good. Mary Ann has her fierce mother face on."

"Who are we talking about?" Liz asked.

Mary Ann wrinkled her nose. "Andrew Carter."

"You say his name like he's the gum stuck to the bottom of your shoe," Renee said.

"I don't like him. I never have."

Liz grinned. "Now you have to tell us."

Renee waved her hand in dismissal. "Andrew and I dated in high school. Long before Josh and I got together."

"And I'm sure he's not the least bit upset Josh is missing."

"Mary Ann! He's not that bad."

"Really? You two haven't spoken in years, and now he shows up?"

"Maybe he's concerned," Opal offered.

"More like making his move," Mary Ann groused.

"Tell us more," Liz prodded.

Renee shrugged. "Not much to tell. We dated for a few years. He was on the football team. Popular. Kind of the big man on campus."

"*After* Josh graduated," Mary Ann interjected.

"Josh and Andrew were always rivals. Mainly in sports but also in other activities at school."

"He never liked Renee and Josh dating," Mary Ann declared.

"So why'd you break up?"

Opal gasped. "Caitlyn!"

"What? It's old news."

"Yes, it is." Renee went quiet for a moment. "Andrew was always selfish, I guess. When things were going good for him, he was the life of the party and we got along great. But if things were bad, he'd be in a foul mood. Our senior year was fun because Andrew didn't have Josh around to make him jealous. But I outgrew him, and I broke things off right after graduation."

"Andrew did not take it well," Mary Ann confirmed.

"No, he didn't. He didn't understand we were over until our first year away at college." Her phone *pinged* again. Renee read the screen and grimaced. "Andrew."

"See," Mary Ann said in a raised tone.

"He's just being nice."

"Nice until he moves in for the kill."

"Josh is the only man for me. If you'll excuse me, I'm going to my room." Renee nearly ran from the living room.

"Has this guy been stalking Renee?" Liz asked Mary Ann.

"Not stalking, bothering. A few texts here and there. Occasionally stopping by unannounced."

Sadie had an "aha" look on her face. "He *is* making his move."

"He might be trying, but Renee only wants to be with Josh." Mary

Ann sighed. "She has put Andrew off in that very gentle way of hers. Too gentle, in my opinion."

The room grew quiet. Liz had to wonder how far Andrew would go to get Renee back. Since Renee was at her most vulnerable, now was the time to strike. She looked across the room. "Sadie, what are you doing for the next week or so?"

"I'll be running interference."

Liz's eyes went wide.

"Yes, I heard you two."

Mary Ann laughed.

"Now what?" Naomi asked Mary Ann. "Do you think Renee should be worried that Andrew had something to do with Josh's disappearance?"

"I don't know. It's no secret that when Renee and Josh started dating Andrew wasn't happy, but they've been together for almost two years. And Andrew has moved on."

"But he still lives here in town?"

"Yes. Renee mentioned that he works for a business downtown, but I never asked what he does."

Liz tapped her lips with her finger. "So if Renee is the rub between the two guys . . ."

"Then maybe we need to watch out for him," Naomi finished.

"Mary Ann, do you have any pictures of Andrew?"

"I might." She went to the hutch and opened the lower door, then pulled out a box. "I have loads of pictures of Renee. He must be in some of them." She sat with the box in her lap and started searching. Before long she found one and handed it to Liz. "It's several years old, but Andrew hasn't changed much."

Liz studied the man in the picture. Tall. Dark hair parted on one side. He had a self-satisfied air about him, taking over the photo, with Renee barely in the frame.

Mary Ann located other pictures and passed them around.

"I've seen him recently," Opal said, squinting at a photo. "Where did I see him?"

"On Main Street?" Sadie asked.

"No."

"At the coffee shop?"

"Maybe . . ."

"We know what he looks like," Liz said. "Keep an eye out."

Mary Ann collected the pictures, and soon, the women packed up to head home.

"Thanks for everything," Mary Ann told her friends. "For a little while we directed Renee's focus on a task other than Josh's disappearance."

Opal hugged her. "He'll turn up. I know it."

The ladies exited and walked down the sidewalk, leaving Liz alone with Mary Ann.

"Well?" Mary Ann asked her.

"I think we have a new lead."

9

It seemed to Liz that she had just caught her breath after the preparations for Renee's wedding and then the chaos following Josh's disappearance when reservations started to pick up and things got busy again. This time of year, with the leaves beginning to change color and a chill biting the air, people wanted a quick getaway. The Olde Mansion Inn filled the bill.

After nearly tripping over Beans multiple times, she refilled his food bowl. As she put the kibble bag away, Sarah entered the kitchen. "Is the Rose of Sharon Room ready?" Liz asked her.

"Yes, I freshened the room and bath."

"Great." Liz perused her reservation list again. "It's only Thursday, and all but one room is booked." She glanced at her employee and grinned. "Nice way to start the weekend."

"Yes." Sarah placed her supply caddy on the granite counter, her fingers lingering along the edge as if she was debating what to do next.

"Is something wrong?"

"I saw Caleb last night, and he is very concerned about Josh's welfare."

Five days had passed, and the police were no closer to finding Josh. It was as though he'd vanished into thin air.

"He's not the only one. Renee is a wreck. It's almost like she's stalled, unable to move from uncertainty toward the future. Even if moving means she looks for Josh herself."

"Do you think she will? Look for Josh, that is?"

"Not in her current state."

Sarah gave her a sly look. "And what about you? Are you jumping in to help?"

"Caleb squealed, didn't he?"

"He only mentioned you spoke to him."

"Guilty. But he wasn't much help."

Sarah stared at her hand and twisted her plain wedding band. "I do not want to imagine how I would feel if anything happened to my Isaac. I almost lost him once, and it was terrible." When she looked up, her eyes were bright with tears. "You have to keep searching."

Liz squeezed her shoulder. "I will."

The morning passed in a flurry of preparations. By early afternoon, Liz needed a break. Maybe a walk would clear her head. She grabbed her purse and a sweater, then called out to Sarah, "I'm going out. Be back in an hour."

The afternoon had warmed but only a bit. It seemed Indian summer had come and gone. Still, the bright blue sky and touch of falling leaves energized her mood. Liz relished the change of seasons. Small-town living had rescued her from the hustle and bustle of her old life in the city when she'd hardly even noticed what time of year it was.

"Yes," she said, inhaling the clean air, "this is so much better."

When Liz reached The Coffee Cup she walked in and ordered a mocha latte. As she waited, she scanned the room. Her gaze stopped on a young man in the corner, busy typing on his smartphone. "Andrew," she whispered.

Now that she saw him in person, she realized she'd run into him before, in fact, right here in the coffee shop. She recalled that when she'd popped in at various times of the day, she had seen him on his phone or talking to someone.

Once she took her coffee from the barista, she headed in his direction. "Excuse me. Andrew Carter?"

He glanced up. "Yes," he said, annoyance in his tone.

She held out her hand. "Liz Eckardt. I own the Olde Mansion Inn."

"Yeah. Right." He returned to his phone, clearly miffed by the interruption.

"Are you friends with Renee Paulson?" Liz hoped her name would grab his attention.

Andrew looked at her. "Is she okay?"

"I wouldn't say okay exactly, but she's hanging in there." Liz took a seat. "Hard to believe Josh is missing. Can't imagine what happened to him."

Andrew's eyes grew dark. "Probably took off."

"I can't see that. Not when he seemed so happy with Renee and apparently had a stable job at the bank."

He pocketed his phone. "Cold feet maybe?"

"Maybe. But he seemed devoted to Renee."

"Then why did he leave her at the altar?" Andrew lifted his chin. "No real man does that."

Liz took a sip of her coffee. "You don't like Josh very much, do you? I was with Renee the other night, and she mentioned that you and Josh aren't friends."

"Josh thinks he's superior to everyone else. Just because he comes from money and is popular doesn't mean he's a great catch. Renee could do better."

"She doesn't see it that way."

"If he's such a wonderful guy, why did he leave? Why does he always take things from me?"

"Take things?" Liz asked. "You mean Renee? It was my understanding you two broke up."

Andrew crossed his arms over his chest. "We did. Mutually. Before we went to college. Doesn't mean I don't still care about her."

Mutually, huh? Not according to Renee. "But you'd rather she wasn't marrying Josh?"

"He's a pain. He hurt Renee and should pay."

Oh my, that sounds serious.

His phone *pinged*, and he glanced down to read a text.

Was Andrew working? He wore a dark suit, which indicated as

much, but why was he in a coffee shop instead of an office in the middle of a workday? "So, what do you do?"

"I'm a financial consultant for a commercial lending company. I help new businesses get off the ground."

"How nice. I'm sure your clients appreciate it."

"Yes. Whatever." Andrew checked his watch. "I gotta go. Meeting a client." He gave her a smug look. "Guess Josh is out of the running on this one."

"You compete for clients?"

"We both have the same kind of job, so yeah, our paths cross."

Liz sipped and waited.

"And before you say it, our competition had nothing to do with Josh leaving."

"Why would I think that?" Liz asked innocently. "I don't know you or the nature of your business with him."

"Josh and I were trying to land the same business loan. Am I glad he's out of the picture? Yeah. But I wouldn't hurt Renee to get the loan."

Andrew might be smarmy, but Liz believed his concern for Renee. He obviously still harbored feelings for her.

He stood. "Get that idea out of your head."

Liz smiled at him. "I had no specific idea."

"Good." Andrew turned and stormed out the door.

Until now.

Andrew and Josh were competitors in business. What new company were they trying to work with? Since Liz wasn't plugged into the business dealings in Pleasant Creek, she had no idea, but she knew someone who would.

She'd head over to Cross Furniture where she was sure to find Jackson this time of day. Swallowing the last of her coffee, she left the shop, nearly colliding with an older man who walked right into her path.

"Whoa, there," he said, grabbing Liz's arms to keep her steady.

"I'm sorry. I didn't see you."

"It's my height. I'm vertically challenged." The man, with a sparse gray comb-over, didn't even meet Liz's eye level. "But the ladies love me anyway."

His statement brought a surprised laugh from Liz. "At least you have confidence."

"In spades." He puffed out his chest. "I'm Curtis Angly. And who might you be?"

"Liz Eckardt. I own the Olde Mansion Inn."

"Ah yes. The bed-and-breakfast. Been meaning to spend a night there, but being on a fixed income puts a knot in my social activities."

Liz had no idea how to respond.

"But for now, I have an appointment to keep."

"Busy man?" Liz teased. For such a busy guy, he wasn't moving.

"You'd think. Life at the senior center keeps me hopping, but once in a while duty calls."

"Good for you."

"Yep, it is good. Wish I had more free time, but at my age, I'm not complaining."

"Curtis, stop lollygagging."

Liz looked over her shoulder to find Betty Hulbert, the woman she'd talked to at the bank, marching their way.

"Watch out," Curtis whispered. "She's a bossy one."

Betty stopped beside them, her irritation evident. "You're going to miss your appointment," she barked.

"It was my fault," Liz cut in. "I ran into Curtis, and we started talking."

"Highlight of my day."

Betty rapped her cane on the sidewalk. "We have important business," she reminded him.

"Don't let me keep you."

Curtis rolled his eyes. "Please keep us."

Liz couldn't help but smile.

Betty tapped her cane again.

"Senior-center business gets boring," he complained.

"Then you shouldn't have volunteered," Betty harrumphed.

"I didn't."

Liz had no idea what they were arguing about, but watching them was worth the price of admission.

A scratchy noise sounded from Betty's oversize purse. She shoved her cane at Curtis and then rummaged through the bag to remove a walkie-talkie. "This is Hummingbird. Come in."

"Abort, abort," an otherworldly voice commanded.

Betty's eyes widened. She dropped the walkie-talkie into her bag and snatched her cane from Curtis. "We should leave."

A van, with *Pleasant Creek Senior Center* painted on the side, inched by. From inside, an older woman frantically waved her arms.

Curtis's expression turned serious. "Nice to meet you," he said to Liz. Then he and Betty rushed off—except they went in the direction Curtis was originally headed, not to the van.

Weird.

Shaking her head, Liz secured her purse strap over her shoulder. It took her only a few minutes to walk to Cross Furniture.

Jackson was standing near the door talking to an employee who was dressed in dark pants and a blue shirt, one of the many Amish men working there.

Jackson's hazel eyes lit up when he saw her. "Liz, what a surprise."

"I hope my dropping by doesn't inconvenience you."

"Not at all." He ushered her to his office, then motioned for her to have a seat. "So tell me, to what do I owe this pleasure?"

"I was wondering about someone, and since you have your finger on the pulse of Pleasant Creek, you seem to be the logical person to ask."

"I guess knowing about the people in town is part of my job as mayor."

"Actually, I was speaking from a business point of view."

Jackson laughed, his tone husky. Since the first time she'd met him, she'd enjoyed the sound. His easygoing personality had made them friends immediately. And the thick brown hair accentuating his handsome face didn't hurt either. "Are you having business troubles?"

"No. More like I'm helping Renee with some things."

His eyes sparkled. "Helping?"

"Okay, snooping. But for a good cause."

"If it's about finding Josh, I'm in."

"Good." She set her purse at her feet. "What can you tell me about Andrew Carter?"

"He works for Integrity Commercial Loan."

"He and Josh are rivals?"

"I guess you could look at it that way. They both secure loans, although Josh handles loans of all kinds at the bank, whereas Andrew mainly works with commercial businesses."

"Do you know anything about a new business coming to town?" Liz asked. "A business that would have Josh and Andrew competing for the loan?"

"There are always new permits coming into town hall. Can you be more specific?"

"I'm afraid not."

Jackson was quiet for a few moments. "The only one I can think of is a merchandise manufacturer. The owners of the company have great plans but no cash. They would be looking for a loan."

"And Josh's bank and Andrew's company are the two contenders?"

"Here in Pleasant Creek, yes."

If Josh and Andrew were after the same business, was it a big enough reason for Andrew to force Josh out of the picture? Maybe get the loan and the girl at the same time? "Thanks. I wanted another opinion of Andrew. You know he and Renee dated in high school?"

"No, but let me guess. Between the loan and Renee, you think he's up to no good?"

"I don't have any actual proof other than he's not the nicest guy."

"A bit into himself?" he said.

"Not Renee's type."

"How's she doing, by the way?"

"Waiting. Hoping. Worrying."

Jackson sighed. "Tough situation. If I can do anything, give me a call."

"Chief Houghton is doing everything he can, but I'll let you know."

They chatted for a few moments. Then Liz rose. "I need to get back to the inn. I have guests checking in."

"And I should get some work done." He escorted her to the door, walking outside with her.

Liz was about to say good-bye when the senior-center van passed. This time there were three occupants. Liz didn't know the woman on the far side of the van, but she recognized Betty, who stared straight ahead, and Curtis, who waved at her from the window.

She waved back.

"Do I want to know?" Jackson asked.

"Just a couple of new friends. They're a bit strange but sweet. I think they like getting out of the senior center once in a while."

"Take my advice. They may seem sweet, but they can be pretty tenacious when they want something."

"You know this from personal experience?"

"Mayoral experience."

She looked at the van with renewed interest. "I'm sure they're harmless."

10

As of Saturday morning, there was still no word on Josh.

Liz hadn't seen Renee, but judging from Mary Ann's worried expression when she came to work at Sew Welcome, things were not good.

Liz scurried around the dining room to replenish a scrambled egg, cheese, and bacon dish. The dining room was filled with guests, which would have usually thrilled her, but she couldn't get her mind off the circumstances. A week had passed since Josh had vanished. The police hadn't discovered any clues. It was like he'd dropped off the face of the earth, as if he'd never existed.

Except many people were grieving his absence.

A loud *psst* disrupted her scattered thoughts.

"Do you have flavored tea bags?" the wife of one of the visiting couples asked Liz. "I don't like plain old tea."

"Let me check." Did she have flavored tea? Her emotions were running high, and she couldn't recall, which bothered her. She prided herself on being in control when running the inn. Josh's disappearance had thrown her off balance.

Carrying the empty platter to the kitchen, she set it on the counter en route to the pantry. Sure enough, she found a box of tea in assorted flavors. Then she remembered Sadie leaving it at the inn.

"Thanks, Sadie," she said. "You're a lifesaver."

"I have been told that a time or two."

Liz whirled around to see Sadie standing behind her. She sported a bright pink visor and big, round sunglasses. "You scared me."

"I do that pretty well too."

"You don't mind if I use a couple of your tea bags, do you?"

"No. I have more stashed in the shop."

"So what's with the glasses?" Liz asked as she removed tea envelopes from the box to place in a decorative container.

"The sun is terribly bright today, so I need them. And they look good." She removed them and turned the glasses sideways to show Liz the crystal-studded earpieces. "They make a fashion statement."

No one had Sadie's fashion sense, which set the woman in a league of her own.

"I came for hot water," Sadie went on. "We had a visitor standing on the doorstep this morning when we opened the shop."

"Who?"

"Mrs. Conrad. Since Josh's disappearance she's been at Sew Welcome every day."

"Maybe she wants company."

"She can't sew, so it has to be the company."

"This is where Josh was going to get married. She must feel a much-needed connection here."

"I agree. So we're keeping her busy. Yesterday I had her do inventory on notions. I believe she actually enjoys counting buttons."

Liz laughed. "The tedious activity probably soothes her."

"Not only that, but she discovered two boxes of thread that I'd forgotten we ordered."

"You forgot something?"

Sadie sniffed. "It does happen on rare occasions."

"To all of us. I'm making more lists than I ever have."

"You're very busy. Lists are a must."

"And so is getting this tea out to my guest." Liz carried the container to the dining room.

Her breakfast guests were gathered around the window. "You don't see that every day," one of the women commented.

"Odd indeed."

Liz couldn't imagine what they were witnessing. Curious, she joined them and looked out the window. Kiera, her part-time gardener, chased the resident bulldog around the side yard. Beans wore a ribbon and a lopsided bow on his head, and he had an object clamped between his teeth.

"Excuse me." Liz dropped the tea beside the coffee carafe on the serving table and rushed outside. "Kiera, what's going on?"

"Beans dug around in the flower bed and got ahold of my bag of bulbs. I can't plant them if he's going to disrupt every place I work."

"He's a dog. He likes to dig."

Jamming her hands on her slim hips, Kiera exuded plenty of attitude for a sixteen-year-old. "And look at the problems it has caused." She referred to the old human remains Beans had unearthed a while back.

"At least he hasn't dug up the lilac bushes again."

Kiera sighed.

"What's with the bow?" Liz grimaced when she recognized it from Renee's wedding decorations. It was a sad reminder of how devastated Renee had been when she canceled the wedding. "I guess someone dropped it while we were cleaning up."

"I noticed him nosing around the garden bench, and when I called out, he took off but not before the ribbon and bow got tangled on his head. When I tried to grab him, the bow twisted to the top."

"He looks like part of a wedding party."

"But dogs don't go to weddings."

Liz was sure some people would argue the point, but she wasn't telling Kiera. "Lucky for you, Beans is usually much too lazy to dig for long." She seized Beans's leash. "I'll take him inside so you can work."

Kiera grabbed the bag Beans had dropped and stomped away.

"What am I going to do with you?" Liz muttered to Beans as she dragged him inside for his beloved bologna snack.

Upon returning to the dining room, she found it cleared out except for Sarah. "Where is everyone?"

"After the show they went to their rooms," Sarah informed her. "It sounded like shopping and sightseeing were next on the list."

Liz surveyed the room. "Well, I guess we can clean up now."

"Why not check if there has been any news about Josh? I can handle this."

"Thanks." Liz removed her apron, then crossed the inn to Sew Welcome. Mary Ann, Sadie, and Mrs. Conrad stood at the counter chatting.

"You should enroll in Miriam's class," Sadie told Mrs. Conrad. "She brings her treadle sewing machine."

"I don't know. I'm not much good with a needle and thread. Put me behind a machine and who knows what will happen."

"You have to start somewhere," Mary Ann said.

"And Miriam is the best," Liz added as she joined them. "You couldn't have more patient guiding hands than hers, Mrs. Conrad."

"Like I told your friends, please call me Elyse."

Liz nodded.

"Miriam's next class is full," Sadie informed Liz. "In fact, two of your guests hired her for a private session this afternoon."

"The reputation of Sew Welcome keeps getting better."

"As it should," Sadie said. "We're serious about our craft."

"Speaking of which . . ." Mary Ann collected a pile of material from the cutting table. "Caitlyn was in last night, and we picked out fabric for the Christmas stockings. Next we need to cut them out."

"Stockings? For what?" Elyse asked.

"Renee's kindergarten class. Their Christmas project," Sadie chimed in. "Stockings for the children at the hospital."

"How sweet. I hope it's more successful than last year. Her class held a fund-raiser for the senior center." Elyse shuddered. "The seniors are a tough crowd. My husband continually has his hands full with them."

Liz thought of Betty and Curtis and smiled. "I met a couple of folks from there recently. They sure seem lively."

"They're always complaining about something. Especially Helen Furst." Elyse glanced at Sadie. "If she ever comes into the shop, you should be worried."

"I'm well aware of Helen. She knows better than to bring her trouble here."

Surprised at Sadie's attitude, Liz asked, "What's the story with Helen?"

"Ringleader," Sadie and Elyse said at the same time.

"What are they up to this time?" Mary Ann asked as she took a pattern book from the shelf.

"They're up in arms about a taco truck. My husband had to shut it down because of a permit problem."

"Tacos on Tires?" Liz asked. "I ate there the other day. The food is fabulous."

"But the owner doesn't take permit issues seriously."

Liz picked up a pair of scissors from the cutting table while Mary Ann unrolled a bolt of festive Christmas fabric.

"We know the judge has an angry business owner and a group of old folks after him." Liz cut into the fabric. "But how serious a problem could the seniors be?" No one answered so she looked up. All eyes were on her.

"Serious enough," Sadie replied. "And furthermore—"

Before she could finish her thought, Renee burst into the store, her cheeks flushed. Liz swore the poor girl had lost at least five pounds, which was quite noticeable on her slender frame.

"What's wrong?" Mary Ann rushed across the room.

"The chief called. He has news. I told him to meet me here." She gripped Mary Ann's hand. "I wanted to be with all of you."

Elyse sank into a nearby chair, her hand over her heart. "Do you think . . . ?"

Sadie placed a gentle hand on her shoulder. "We'll know soon."

Five minutes later Chief Houghton arrived, his face void of emotion. He carried a plastic evidence bag.

This can't be good, Liz thought but immediately brushed her negativity aside.

Renee composed herself and walked across the room to meet the chief. "Josh?"

"We haven't located him. But we found his cell phone." He held out the bag.

Renee reached out, curling her fingers into a ball just before touching the plastic. She swallowed, then took the bag. "It looks like Josh's phone."

"After we dusted it for prints, the tech checked. It's Josh's."

Renee shivered.

"Where did you find it?" Elyse asked as she put her arm around Renee.

"Out on county road 450. It was in a drainage ditch."

The road to Miriam's place. And Caleb's.

"We talked to some of the residents nearby, but we keep getting the same story. No one saw Josh Saturday morning."

"But we know he went to see Caleb," Liz corrected.

"Yes," the chief said. "*We* do."

Liz bit her lower lip.

"Can you tell from any of the calls where he might be?" Renee asked the chief.

"We're still working on it."

"May we keep the phone?" Elyse asked in a halting voice.

"I'm sorry, but no. It's evidence."

And just like that, the hopeful mood of the room deflated.

Renee handed the bag back to the chief. "What happens now?"

"We keep searching."

"Isn't the fact that you found his phone here in Pleasant Creek a good sign?" Liz asked.

"This is an ongoing investigation," Chief Houghton stated. "I can't answer that question."

Or didn't want to.

"We appreciate whatever you can tell us," Elyse said. She sounded calm, as opposed to her anxiousness when Josh had first gone missing. Hanging around Sew Welcome seemed to have grounded her.

"It's been a week," Renee whispered. "That can't be a good thing."

Liz glimpsed a flash of sympathy in the chief's eyes. They all knew that the longer Josh was gone without a trail to follow, the harder it might be to find him. Time was the enemy right now.

"My men and I are taking this investigation seriously," the chief assured them. "I've asked you this before, Renee, but do you recall if Josh was having trouble with anyone?"

She brushed her hair from her eyes. "I don't know. I was too focused on the wedding."

"Mrs. Conrad?"

"He didn't say a word about any trouble." She paused. "Although he did say that once he took care of this new loan application, the pressure would be off. I don't know what he meant."

The chief held up the bag. "Thank you, ladies. I'm going back to the station to see if there are any updates."

Elyse stepped forward. "You will call us if you learn anything new?"

"Of course." The chief headed to the door.

Before he exited the shop, Renee ran to him. "Chief?"

He turned.

"His last call. Was it . . . Did he call me?"

The chief hesitated, then said, "Josh's last call was to Andrew Carter."

11

"Andrew?" Renee stumbled back. "That doesn't make sense. Why would Josh call him?"

"The department is investigating the matter," Chief Houghton answered, but one look at Renee's stricken face and the normally tough chief seemed to crumble. "I know you're upset. Please bear with us. We're doing everything we can."

"Okay, I . . ." Renee tucked her hair behind one ear. "I guess I'd hoped he was thinking of me on our wedding day."

Mary Ann put her arm around Renee's shoulder.

Renee teared up. "Aren't I just awful, feeling sorry for myself when Josh is missing?" She glanced at Elyse. "Of course you're as worried as I am."

Elyse grabbed a tissue and handed it to her once future daughter-in-law. "Please don't be so hard on yourself. We all want Josh to come home safe and sound, but I also understand you'd hoped his mind was on you."

Renee sniffed. "Thanks." She shook off her tears. "I should get going. There are things I need to do."

Silence filled the room after she left.

The chief cleared his throat. "I'm leaving as well."

"Let me walk you out." Liz led the chief to the front door.

Once they were on the porch, Liz said, "I didn't want to upset Renee, but I ran into Andrew at the coffee shop the other day. He told me that sometimes he and Josh compete for business loans. In fact, he didn't seem too broken up over the fact that Josh went missing and he had a better shot at a deal they were both after."

"I spoke to Carter and got the same impression. But just because I don't think much of the man personally doesn't mean he's behind the disappearance."

No, it didn't, but she couldn't forget Andrew's sneer and lack of concern for Josh's welfare. Anyone with a bit of compassion would have shown some sympathy.

A gust of wind blew leaves in a frenzy about the sidewalk. Liz rubbed her arms against the chill. "I know. Like everyone, I'm worried about so much time passing and no leads at all."

"Believe it or not, my department is doing everything we can to find Josh. He is our top priority."

"I'm glad to hear that, not that I doubted your efforts." She sighed. "Every time I see Renee I hope you guys have a breakthrough. And not only for her sake but for his parents as well."

"It looks like Mrs. Conrad is in good hands with Mary Ann and Sadie. As for Renee, all I can suggest is continued support, which I can see you're giving."

"And the judge?"

"He has plenty on his plate right now."

"What does—?"

The chief held up his hand. "We're on it, okay?"

Liz bit her tongue. He wasn't going to say anything more. No point in pushing the man. "Thank you, Chief Houghton."

He nodded and jogged down the steps.

Liz watched until he reached his patrol car. Before she went back inside, a black buggy stopped in front of the inn. Miriam spoke to her husband, then got out and headed up the sidewalk.

"Was that Chief Houghton I saw drive away?" she asked when she reached Liz.

"Yes. He came with news. Someone discovered Josh's cell phone."

A wrinkle furrowed Miriam's brow. "Yes, I know."

"You do? How?"

"Caleb found it. He turned it over to Bishop Manz, who gave it to the police."

"I'm surprised."

"We do not normally get involved with your investigations, but from what I understand, Caleb begged the bishop to hand over the phone. I think this entire situation concerning Josh bothers Caleb deeply."

"I agree."

Miriam looked troubled. "I also understand you spoke to Caleb after leaving the farm."

"I bumped into him on the way home."

"If by 'bumped into' you mean 'followed,' then, yes, you did."

"I didn't mean to cause Caleb any problems."

"He is truly worried and wants to help. While the bishop did not like him speaking to you, he understood. Josh may not be a part of the Amish community, but his friendship with Caleb is long-standing."

"I promised Caleb I wouldn't say a word to anyone, and I haven't."

Miriam touched Liz's shoulder. "Caleb is a *guta* young man."

"So is Josh."

"Then we continue to pray."

Liz clutched Miriam's hand. "On that we can agree."

They moved inside to escape the blustering wind, chatting as they entered Sew Welcome. Miriam's students hovered near the fabric section as Mary Ann cut a section of bright printed cloth and Sadie set Elyse up with a new task.

Seeing everyone busy, Liz turned to leave.

Miriam stopped her. "Do you have a moment?"

"Sure. What's going on?"

Miriam searched her bag, then removed a pieced square of fabric and gave it to Liz. "Grace finished the first block of her quilt. She is very excited and asked me to show it to you."

In the quilt block, Liz recognized the fabric remnants she'd dropped off at the farm. The pieces were geometric in shape. When Liz flipped it over, she admired the precise stitches made by the talented twelve-year-old. "I'm impressed. Most adults can't sew a block together this well."

"I know I am her mother, but I cannot help but be pleased by her work."

Liz handed the block back. "Tell her I'm looking forward to seeing the completed quilt."

Miriam studied the piece and beamed. "I will be sure to tell her."

Liz returned to the kitchen. Sarah had the kitchen cleanup well in hand. As Liz went upstairs to tidy the rooms while the guests were out, she couldn't stop replaying the chief's words. Judge Conrad had more problems? A missing son would rate high on the list, but since Liz had spoken to the man, she knew he could add a few more items to said list, like a vehicle with brake failure and people not happy with his legal decisions. Could all of this be tied to Josh's disappearance? For the life of her, she couldn't link the pieces.

By late afternoon, Liz was still unable to shake the heavy feeling that something was off. She set out cookies and warm beverages for her guests. After a busy day out and about, a few of them engaged her in small talk in the sitting room, admiring the decor, the inn, and Pleasant Creek in general. She loved visiting with her guests, always curious about their lives and occupations, but today, she was glad when they returned to their rooms.

In her private quarters, Liz booted up her laptop. She searched for local legal cases that were public record, and once she found them, she dived right in.

She immediately found the citations Pete Hardy had racked up. Just as Jackson had told her, the man hadn't met a permit he didn't violate. Could he have been the one to sabotage the judge's brakes? He seemed angry enough. And if so, what did he expect to gain? Then there was his difficulty of making loan payments. It seemed to be common knowledge since Pete had no problem announcing his situation to the public. How did Josh fit into this scenario? Was Pete an irate customer seeking revenge? At this point, there was no telling.

Next, Liz pulled up the website of the local newspaper, *Pleasant Creek News & Views*. She scanned articles, searching for any references to the judge or the taco truck. Before long she found a story about a group of folks from the senior center holding a sit-in at the courthouse. She grinned at a photo of seniors, some in wheelchairs, others holding signs that read Free Tacos on Tires.

The fact that Pete's self-induced permit problems had caused their outrage didn't seem to matter; the seniors wanted their tacos and would go to great lengths to get them. Apparently, Pete's legal problems kept him from stopping by the center on his regular day. Worse, when the truck was out of commission, they missed out on cheap food.

Liz pictured the outspoken characters she'd recently met: Curtis, the flirt, and Betty with her cane and code name. Who had a code name? Liz could see them causing trouble, especially for the judge or anyone who made them unhappy, but she couldn't imagine them deliberately cutting brake lines. Still, there was a connection. One she needed to check out.

She grabbed her phone and speed-dialed Naomi. "What are you doing after you close the bakery?"

"Not much. Catching up on laundry, tidying the house, that sort of thing."

"How would you like to go to the senior center with me?"

"What on earth for?"

"I have a feeling the seniors are up to something." She explained running into Curtis and Betty and their odd mission in town.

Naomi laughed. "Now you've made me curious. I'm in."

The two met up an hour later. Both had dressed warmly, Liz in an emerald-green sweater, jacket, and jeans and Naomi in a pink T-shirt and matching fleece jacket and black slacks. Liz drove to an address a few blocks off Main Street. The sprawling one-story senior center was a part-residential, part-community center for folks over sixty-five. As Liz pulled into the parking lot, she noticed the grounds were well maintained, and the building appeared freshly painted. There were benches flanking the front door and a few more scattered around the lawn and under mature maple and oak trees.

"I called ahead to see if there are any special activities going on," Liz said. "It's karaoke night."

"Sounds fun."

"If the two folks I've already met are there, it will be interesting."

After parking, they walked into the building and stopped in the foyer.

"I wonder which way we should go," Liz said.

"East," came a disembodied voice.

Liz looked around. "Excuse me?"

Nearly hidden in the shadows sat a gentleman in a lawn chair. "You're lookin' for the singers, right?" He pointed to her left. "East. Thataway."

"Thanks. And you are?"

"Burns. Colonel Burns. United States Army. Retired."

"Nice to meet you. I'm Liz and this is—"

"Naomi Mason," he finished. "Owns the bakery. I really like your shortbread cookies. And you're Liz Eckardt, owner of the Olde Mansion Inn. I know the lay of the town."

"Pleased to meet you," Naomi said.

"The others are in the Earl Daniels Dayroom for Special Activities. EDDSA for short."

"The dayroom. Got it." Liz sniffed the air. "Do you smell smoke?"

Naomi sniffed as well. "Is that a cigar?"

"Yes, ma'am." He moved his previously hidden hand and held up a lit cigar. "Too cold to go outside so I sneak a smoke by the front door." He cocked his head. "Our secret, ladies?"

"I suppose, although you know smoking isn't good for you."

"Neither was dodgin' bullets overseas, but I did it anyway. Way I see it, I deserve a vice or two in my old age." He settled back in his chair.

Liz wasn't about to argue. "Thank you. We'll be going."

They'd taken only a few steps when they heard music.

"I'd say we're heading in the right direction," Naomi said.

They turned a corner and entered a large, brightly lit room with people seated around half a dozen tables. On a small stage at one end of the room a white-haired man pushed some buttons on a karaoke machine, and a man and woman hurried up the steps and huddled behind the microphone as the music began. The woman giggled and waved at the crowd, and she and her partner went into an enthusiastic rendition of "Don't Go Breaking My Heart."

Liz and Naomi sat at a table with two empty seats, turning their chairs to watch the couple sing and flirt their hearts out.

"That was surprisingly good," Naomi commented as the song ended and applause erupted around them.

"What were you expecting, off-key and growly? We don't let just anyone up on that stage."

Liz looked over her shoulder, straight into the indignant face of Betty Hulbert who sat at the same table. She wore a floral-print dress, and her hair was permed tightly. "Betty, I'm glad to see you."

"Really?" she huffed. "Doesn't seem like it."

"I didn't mean to sound judgmental," Naomi said. "But anytime I've been at a place with karaoke singers, it's usually awful."

Betty's expression softened. "That is true. We vet our singers to ensure they can hold a tune. Most folks have to turn up their hearing aids, so we make it worth their while."

"You have a packed house," Liz observed.

"Not much else to do on a Saturday night." Betty narrowed her eyes. "So what are you two women doing here when you should be out on dates or at least partying?"

Liz nearly choked. "We don't exactly party."

"And we aren't dating anyone," Naomi answered.

"Got some single fellas here we can fix you up with."

"That's okay," they both replied.

Betty shrugged. "Your loss."

Liz laughed. "I appreciate your concern, but honestly, after meeting you and Curtis, I was curious about where you live."

"Curtis," Betty said in exasperation. "Watch out for that one."

"I enjoyed talking to him, but he seemed to be in a hurry. Actually you both did. Hummingbird, was it?"

Squirming in her chair, Betty tapped her cane on the tile floor, not meeting Liz's eyes.

Another gentleman grabbed the microphone, launching into a rap rendition of "New York, New York." By the time he finished with a resounding crescendo, Betty had pulled herself together.

"So," Liz reminded her, "were you two on a mission?"

"Senior business. That's all you need to know."

Before Liz could ask another question, Curtis called her name. Grinning from ear to ear, he scurried to her table. Tonight he wore a jacket, a shirt and tie, and sharply creased slacks.

Liz stood. "Curtis, what a place you have here."

"It's not the grand ballroom at the Drake Hotel, but it works for us." He smiled at Naomi. "And who's your lovely friend?"

Liz made introductions, and soon a few other seniors joined them.

"How'd you find us?"

"The colonel sent us this way," Naomi said.

"Isn't he dreamy?" A woman with purplish hair and even darker purple eye shadow sighed.

"Ah, sure." Liz smiled at the woman, then turned her attention to Curtis. "This is a lively group."

"You bet. Karaoke is the big night around here, but we also have game nights, book clubs, and dancing once a month."

"That's quite a schedule." Naomi turned to Liz. "They socialize more than we do."

Curtis squinted at Naomi. "You own the bakery, right?"

"Sweet Everything."

"Next time I'm in the area I'll stop in."

"Please do."

"Maybe we can hold some kind of baking class here," Liz suggested. "You know, in addition to your other activities."

"Now that would bring a crowd," Betty chimed in. "Especially if we can eat. Our usual cook isn't all that picky about what he prepares for us."

Curtis nodded. "That means we're always looking for other ways to get variety."

"Do you have special food days?"

"Wednesday tacos," the group replied in unison.

Bingo, Liz thought. "Now that sounds festive."

Betty frowned. "Except when the truck can't make it here. Which is often."

"The truck?"

"Tacos on Tires," Curtis piped up.

Liz glanced at Naomi. "Sure, I've heard of it. Why I just—"

"Curtis," another lady hissed.

Curtis waved her away. "That's right. Pete knows how to make tacos the way we like them. Not too spicy—"

The group enthusiastically agreed.

"—since our constitutions can't handle it but tasty and easy on the stomach."

Was that even possible? Yet from what Liz had tasted, Pete had a golden touch with tacos.

"Unlike Mutt, who is merely a cook and not even a tiny bit passionate about his art," Betty grumbled. "At least Pete cares about us."

"And he gives us a special rate," a man said, his comb-over lifting from his scalp. "We're on a fixed income, you know."

"Since he gives us a break, we're supportive." Curtis lifted his shoulder. "If it weren't for some legal mess he landed himself in, we'd be seeing him more often. If I've told him once, I've told him plenty of times, don't—"

"Curtis! What's going on?" A tall, big-boned woman with glasses, dressed in a flowing blouse, black polyester pants, and orthopedic shoes, marched toward them. By the thunderous look on her face, things were about to get downright serious.

12

Liz retreated as the furious woman approached, colliding with Naomi. "Sorry. She startled me."

Naomi regarded the stern woman and gulped. "No apology needed."

"And who would you two be?" the woman questioned in a voice of steel. Liz licked her lips. "Liz Eckardt. And this is my friend Naomi."

Naomi gave a weak wave.

"Who are you here to see?"

"Why, me, of course," Curtis declared.

The woman scowled at him. "You didn't tell me."

"And you're not the boss of me."

Goodness. The heavy tension was more suited to adolescents than seniors. "And you are?" Liz asked, forcing a smile.

"Helen Furst."

Ah. The woman Sadie had mentioned in not-so-glowing terms. "I hope you don't mind us crashing your party."

"We don't get many visitors from the outside."

A chorus of agreement followed.

"We should change that," Liz offered, saddened by the woman's comment, despite her underlying mission.

Helen stared Liz down, her glasses magnifying her eyes.

Liz squirmed uncomfortably. She felt like a trespasser being interrogated without the benefit of legal counsel. And since she'd been legal counsel once, she didn't like the insinuation that she'd done something wrong by coming here to visit. Sure, she had ulterior motives, but Helen wasn't privy to them.

If she wasn't surrounded by at least twenty-five other people, Liz might have bolted right then and there, which made her even more annoyed. Helen couldn't be a day under seventy, and the woman clearly ran a tight ship.

Liz swallowed. Waited.

Finally, Helen's intense expression relaxed. "We don't discuss senior business with strangers."

"They aren't strangers," Curtis told her.

"They are to me."

"Well, you don't run the joint either."

Helen glared at Curtis, as if he was totally mistaken in his assessment of her place in the senior-center hierarchy. The two were at a standoff.

Helen eventually backed down. "Sorry. It's unusual for guests to attend our activities. People make promises, then don't show up."

Liz could certainly understand her disappointment. When older folks were forgotten, it had to hurt. For that reason alone, Liz would cut her a little slack. "Curtis was telling us about the goings-on here. They sound fun."

"We make do." Helen's voice remained frosty.

Naomi tugged on Liz's sleeve. "Tell her about the baking class."

"The what?" Helen demanded, not missing a thing.

"We want to offer a baking class or at least schedule a time to bake goodies for the residents."

Helen's face softened a little. "You'd have to take that up with the director. Was there anything else?"

"Yes. The girls are going to sing for us," Curtis said with a wink.

Liz coughed. "Oh no, we'll pass."

"Then why bother coming by?" Helen asked.

Liz opened her mouth to explain but decided against it. It was time to leave. Helen was sharp and on the defensive. Besides, she'd gotten enough information for now. The seniors had issues with their meals, and that explained why they rallied around Pete and his food truck.

"Naomi and I need to get going." Liz inched away. "Hopefully, we'll be back soon."

"See you again." Naomi waved.

Helen glared at them.

The group said good-bye, with Curtis promising to be in the front row for the baking activity.

Liz caught a worried look on Betty's face, but it quickly vanished. *Strange.*

"Oh my," Naomi panted as they darted down the empty hallway. "That woman was downright scary."

"And hiding something."

"You think?"

"I saw the lady who tried to stop Curtis from talking about the taco truck slip away when he ignored her. She returned with the group trailing Helen."

"What was up with Helen? You'd think she'd be happy to have visitors."

Liz nodded. "Instead, she chose to make us uncomfortable."

"I wonder why."

"I'm sure we'll find out when we return for our baking date."

"I'm amazed at how your mind works," Naomi teased.

"It's a gift."

They both chuckled as they came upon the colonel, still sitting sentinel.

"You ladies leaving so soon?"

"Yes, but we'll be back."

He raised his bushy brows.

"To bake," Naomi clarified.

"Sweets." The colonel grinned. "Another of my vices."

"Curtis said something about not tolerating spicy food," Liz said.

"Yep, but Pete knows how to take care of us. He promised to set up a satellite kitchen here if he wins the next competition. Then we can boot out the current cook."

"Pete's food is amazing."

"That's why he wins. Course, he can't manage his affairs worth a darn. He needs help."

"Your help?"

The colonel shrugged. "Anyone's help."

"I see." Liz buttoned her jacket. "Good night."

The evening had dissipated into murky shadows. As Liz and Naomi walked to the car, wind-tossed leaves created a colorful tapestry beneath their feet. Burning wood scented the air, and Liz imagined taking advantage of the fireplace at the inn. If her guests were in for the night, she'd make the sitting room cozy.

"So," Naomi said, her features mottled by shadow as they moved under the lights in the parking lot, "I take it I need to come up with a recipe or two?"

"If we have any hope of figuring out what's going on here, you'd better pull out your best recipes. In the meantime, I'll visit a certain food-truck owner to see how the seniors plan to help him out of his legal mess."

Late Monday morning, Liz called the senior center. The director was thrilled with her suggestion of a baking event. Liz decided to leave the particulars to Naomi because it was her area of expertise.

When she called Naomi with the news, her friend was ecstatic. "I got up early this morning with lots of ideas. I'll call the center to find out if there are any dietary restrictions."

"They eat semi-spicy tacos. How many restrictions can there be?"

Naomi chuckled. "I'll get the supplies and set us up to visit Tuesday morning."

"Sounds like a plan."

After giving Sarah instructions for the day and patting Beans on the head, Liz drove out to Pete's property. She rumbled down the long, unkempt driveway. The two-story house needed painting, but it appeared sturdy enough. The grass was mostly brown, with scattered dirt patches. From what she could tell, the expanse of land went on for a good distance. There were areas of trees clumped together, random bushes, and many abandoned cars in various states of disrepair. This must be what junkyard heaven looked like.

The food truck was parked on one side of the house near a dilapidated garage. She stopped near it and exited her car. As she approached, she noticed denim-clad legs sticking out from under the truck. Then a body rolled out from underneath.

Pete stood, a fierce look marring his face, and dropped the tool he'd been holding. He fished around in his back pocket, producing a red rag, and wiped his hands as he stomped over to her. "Here to accuse me again?" His surly mood hadn't improved since the last time she'd talked to him.

"Sorry. I had that coming," Liz admitted. "No. I want to talk to you about the residents at the senior center."

"They okay?"

"Yes. I saw them the other night. Apparently, you're their hero."

A grudging smile—well, she supposed it was a smile—graced his lips. "They're my biggest supporters."

"At the food-truck competitions?"

"Yeah." Pete grinned. "Just last month a bunch of 'em took the van to a competition in Fort Wayne. They camped out in lawn chairs and watched all day, cheering whenever I advanced to the next round."

"They seem pretty loyal."

"One of 'em even tried to bribe a judge. Thankfully, the official thought it was a prank. Problem was, the old dude meant it."

"I got the impression they want to help you. With your legal troubles, that is."

He stilled. "Got a problem with that?"

"No. I think it's sweet." Despite Pete's gruff exterior, the seniors had decided to back him in his culinary endeavors. It made Liz love them more.

"What do you really want? I told you I don't know anything about Josh."

"I thought maybe you might have noticed something odd when you saw him at the bank. The police don't have any leads, and Renee is beyond worried."

Pete gestured to the truck. "If you want to talk, you gotta do it around my work. It's maintenance day."

As they walked toward the food truck, Liz tilted her head to study the vehicle. The paint was spotless, the tires shiny. She noticed a wrench thingy on the ground along with a black bottle. "Changing the oil?"

"Yep. Gotta keep this beauty running smooth."

Admirable. From the looks of it, Pete took better care of his truck than the rest of his property.

He got down on the creeper and slid under the truck once again. "I told the police chief I didn't see anything weird and that I haven't talked to Josh since we argued over my late-payment history."

"He had to ask."

"Then he accused me of cutting the judge's brake lines. Like I have time for messing with his car."

"I've talked to as many people as I can think of," Liz said. "No one knows anything. It's like Josh vanished."

"Sorry about him missing his wedding, but like I told everyone, I don't know anything."

"You did have it out for him."

Pete rolled out and skewered her with an indignant look. "I don't need to hurt the guy. I'm gonna get caught up on the payments. Pay the fines." He reached under the truck, pulled out a pan filled with greasy oil, and shoved it out of the way. "I got me a private sponsor."

"Good news. Who is it?"

"It's private," he snapped. "They don't want their name to take away from the truck."

Wasn't the point of sponsorship to get your name before the

public? Liz supposed some backers wanted to remain anonymous, but she found the idea odd.

"Now I can enter the big show in Chicago." Pete started to walk away. "Follow me. I gotta get a turn-signal lens from a truck out back."

"So, the big show?" Liz prompted as she tiptoed through the clumpy grass. When she'd slipped on ballet flats this morning, she hadn't envisioned herself trudging through the back forty.

"If I win this one, I'll get all kinds of endorsements. A national tour. Franchising. I'll finally make it. Maybe even open my own headquarters."

"I hadn't realized food trucks were such a big business."

Pete stopped to inspect a van, decided against the part, and moved on. "It can be life changing when you get the right attention."

Liz stepped over discarded parts. The hem of her jeans snagged on the ragged edge of a metal bumper. "I wish you the best. And I'm sorry for bugging you. I just hoped you remembered something."

"If I do I'll call the chief." He crouched down and pried a red cover off the back of a disabled truck.

"I'll leave you alone so you can finish up. Hope the competition goes well."

"I'm making sure it will."

As Pete worked on the lens, Liz turned to walk back to her car. She skirted a red sedan and nearly tripped over a . . . What was that? A big chunk of a metal engine. As she steadied herself, she glimpsed a silver car partially covered by a black tarp, like the wind had displaced it. She moved closer and took a deep breath when she spotted a sticker on the back bumper. *Purdue University. Josh's alma mater.*

Liz whipped off the cover completely and peered inside the window. There was a tuxedo jacket on the passenger seat. Her hand flew to her mouth.

"Hey! What're you doing over there? Get away or you might get hurt."

She whirled around and pointed at the car. "You said you didn't have anything to do with Josh's disappearance. What's his car doing here?"

"That's not Josh's car."

"Really? Take a look."

Pete pocketed the lens and plodded over, his face flushed. He peeked through the window on the other side of the car. A few seconds later his head popped up. She watched his face go white. "This is Josh's car."

"What did you do?"

"Nothing." His voice rose. "I didn't put it here."

"Then how do you explain it?"

"My buddies dump their junkers here all the time." Pete ran a shaking hand through his hair. "Honestly, somebody could have left it, and I'd never know the difference."

"You expect me to believe you?"

"Why would I take Josh's car?"

"You were angry with him. And his father. Payback is my first thought."

"No way! And jeopardize going to the competition?"

Liz opened the car door and stuck her head inside. She gasped and staggered back. Then met Pete's confused gaze. "There's blood on the driver's seat."

13

After calling the police, Liz moved far away from the car, and Pete wisely did the same. They waited by the food truck.

A patrol car pulled up, and Officer Jack Gerst stepped out, his boyish face a mask of seriousness. "The chief is on the way," he said in greeting. "Show me the vehicle."

Liz led the way, with Pete trailing. She had to admit that he seemed legitimately upset. Could his explanation be true? That someone had hidden Josh's car on the property and Pete had no clue?

They reached the vehicle, and the officer inspected the area.

"I noticed blood on the driver's seat," Liz offered.

Officer Gerst glanced at Liz as he pulled a pair of latex gloves from his pants pocket. "Did you touch anything?"

"Only the door when I opened it."

Pete's voice sounded strangled when he said, "I didn't touch anything."

A bird hopped from branch to branch on an overhanging tree limb, as if trying to get closer to the action. Liz shivered, not from the cold but from envisioning the blood on the seat.

Another car sped up the driveway. Soon Chief Houghton joined them. "Josh's car?"

Liz nodded.

The chief pierced Pete with his gaze. "We need to talk."

The chief and Pete walked away.

Liz barely breathed as Officer Gerst meticulously searched the car. After a few minutes he walked to Liz.

"Is that Josh's blood?" she whispered.

"I can't say for sure. I need to call forensics."

Liz's heart beat rapidly. How were Renee and Josh's parents

going to handle this latest news? As far as leads went, this was the worst-case scenario.

Then a crime-scene van arrived. As much as she wanted to stick around, Liz knew there was nothing she could do. The police had to investigate, and she, along with everyone else, had to wait for answers.

"Liz?"

She faced the chief.

"Care to tell me your version of the events?"

She gathered her thoughts and explained why she'd come to talk to Pete, their conversation, and how she found the car.

He took notes. "Pete said pretty much the same."

"Now what?"

"Now you go home. Let us do our job."

"Are you going to tell Renee?"

The chief met her gaze, his eyes troubled. "I'm heading to Mary Ann's. Then I'll go by the Conrads' house."

"Can I—?"

"Tell the others? This will get out soon enough, so please keep it contained to your small group for now."

"I will," Liz said, then stumbled to her car on unsteady legs. Once she was seated behind the wheel, the tears she'd been fighting stung with a vengeance. She allowed them to roll down her cheeks as she let her emotions go. Poor Josh. They'd found his phone and his car and . . . blood. Would his body be next?

Don't think like that, she admonished herself, roughly brushing the tears from her face. She wouldn't believe Josh might be dead. After all, he wasn't in the vehicle. There was still hope.

Finally, Liz started the car and returned to the inn. She tried to compose herself before entering Sew Welcome, but one look at her made Mary Ann and Sadie stop in their tracks.

"It's Josh," Mary Ann whispered.

"Indirectly. I found his car on Pete Hardy's property. Josh wasn't inside."

The two women watched her with wide eyes.

"There was blood on the driver's seat."

Mary Ann slumped against the sales counter. Sadie wrapped her arm around Mary Ann's waist, then led her to a nearby chair.

"I called the police. They're handling it."

"What was his car doing there?" Sadie asked.

"I don't know." Liz relayed the events of her visit. "Pete was as surprised as me."

Sadie glanced down at Mary Ann. "Josh wasn't there. That's good." She tried to put a positive spin on the situation, but it didn't quite reach her voice.

"He's still missing," Liz stated the obvious.

"This is going to destroy Renee. This . . . this— " With eyes wild, Mary Ann jumped up. "I have to get back home." She rushed behind the counter and grabbed her purse. "She has to be told the latest development."

"When I left, the chief was heading over to tell her."

"I need to hurry." Mary Ann fished her keys out of her purse.

Sadie snatched them from her hand. "Mary Ann Berne, there is no way I'm letting you drive in this state. I love my business partner, so I'm taking you home."

"Fine. Let's get going."

Sadie glanced at Liz. "Hold down the fort?"

"Sure. I'll ask Sarah to stay at the inn a little later while I keep an eye on the shop."

As Mary Ann flew out the door, Sadie held her thumb and pinkie by her ear and mouth in the universal sign of "Call me."

"If I hear anything." Liz stood by the open door until the Sew Welcome van tore out of the parking lot. "Be careful," she whispered, offering up a silent prayer.

Sarah was in the kitchen at the sink, rinsing out a glass. She looked up when Liz entered the room. "Are you okay?"

"I will be." Liz retrieved a glass from the cabinet and poured iced tea from the fridge into it. After a long drink, she said, "I found Josh's car."

Sarah pressed her hand to her stomach. "And Josh?"

Liz shook her head. "There was blood inside."

"Oh my," Sarah whispered, taking a seat on one of the stools. "What happens now?"

"The police keep investigating."

Sarah picked at the seam of her apron. "What if there's more?"

"More?"

"Yes." Sarah paused, as if weighing her words. "The other day when I was carrying a laundry basket to the kitchen I overheard Isaac and Caleb discussing Josh. I did not mean to listen."

Liz leaned back against the counter. "What did they say? Was it important?"

"I believe so. Caleb said there is more to Josh's disappearance than just a banking problem. He said Josh was checking into it, and Caleb wondered if that was why he went missing. I do not know what *it* is."

Rubbing her temple, Liz sighed. "And I take it neither of the men elaborated."

"I am afraid not. They stopped talking when Isaac noticed me."

"Every time we turn around it's something new. Unfortunately, you didn't get the rest of the conversation, so whatever *it* is will stay a secret because I doubt Caleb will confide in me."

"I wanted to bring it up to Isaac, but you know our ways."

"Do you think you could convince Isaac to report what Caleb knows? Maybe there's a way for Caleb to inform the police without causing problems in your community."

"I cannot promise, but I will ask. If anyone understands the importance of people coming forward with the truth, it is Isaac."

"Thanks. Whatever *it* is, it's bound to come out at some point. The truth always does."

Sarah jumped from the stool. "I have finished for the day. I should get home."

"Do you mind waiting until Sadie gets back? She took Mary Ann home and asked me to keep an eye on the store."

"I will prepare the afternoon snack."

"Great." Liz hoped Sadie would return before the afternoon snack hour so Liz could catch up with her guests. Only two retired couples remained from the weekend. She wanted to hear how the visit was going and also about their sewing lessons, which reminded her, she still had to complete her share of the stocking cutouts for the Christmas project.

Two more rooms were booked for Thursday through Sunday and another two for the weekend. With an almost full house, Liz had plenty to keep her busy, but she found herself staring out the window of Sew Welcome. Discovering Josh's car had rattled her more than she anticipated. She shoved away her musings and searched for the Christmas fabric.

The front door slammed. Shoppers? Perhaps Sadie back from dropping off Mary Ann? She turned, surprised when Jackson entered the room.

Dressed in a casual caramel-colored sweater and tan slacks, he halted when he saw her, his eyes filled with concern. "I just heard the latest news."

"Then you know Josh is still missing."

"Yes." He ran his fingers through his short hair. "The more time we spend trying to find him . . ."

"The less our chances of success," Liz finished.

"I'd say your discovery has really upped the efforts of the police department." Jackson moved closer.

Liz realized she was very glad he'd stopped by. She valued his ready ear and wise observations. "I'm sure finding blood has motivated the troops. And since most everyone in town knows Josh, they're working overtime."

"Still, it feels like everything is a dead end."

Liz considered mentioning her conversation with Sarah, but what was the point? If she learned anything later on, she could always fill him in. Instead, she went in a different direction. "Were you able to find out about the new business we talked about?"

"Yes. W&K Quality Merchandise and Manufacturing is a company that produces promotional supplies, like T-shirts, cups with company logos, pens, that sort of thing. They operate out of Chicago, but they're relocating the entire operation here."

"So that means jobs for Pleasant Creek?"

"If it happens, yes. I understand the plan is to move the plant into a bigger facility and upgrade their Web presence to distribute their products."

"I don't know what I'd hoped for, but a manufacturing company is not it."

"Why not?" he asked.

"That type of company doesn't have anything to do with the judge, food trucks, or retired people."

"Come again?"

"Pete has a big following from the senior center. Naomi and I are going over there tomorrow to bake and coax out secrets."

"Why am I not surprised?"

Liz pursed her lips. "There's something going on over there. I can feel it."

"Something that may shed light on what happened to Josh?"

"We'll find out."

"Look, if you need anything, you know where to find me."

"Yes, busy with the city or your furniture company. You certainly don't need to worry about whatever I get into."

Jackson grinned. "Maybe I like knowing what you're into."

Before either could say another word, the front door slammed again and Sadie walked into the store. "Oh," she said after viewing the two of them together, "I see you have company."

"Jackson heard about Josh's car and wanted to check on me."

"Sure he did."

Liz nearly sputtered at Sadie's sly expression.

"On that note, I'm off." Jackson looked at Liz. "Call me."

"I will."

"Let me guess," Sadie said as she removed her jacket and stored it and her purse behind the counter. "He heard about the blood."

"I bet most of Pleasant Creek has heard by now."

"Yet no one knows a thing. Odd for a small town."

"Can I ask you a question?"

Sadie pushed up the sleeves of her pink blouse. "Fire away."

"The senior center. What's your take?"

"Helen Furst believes she's in charge."

"That's my impression too."

"Even when we were young, she always had a group of girls at her beck and call."

"Still does," Liz said.

"So what's your concern about Helen?"

"I can't put my finger on it. When Naomi and I stopped there the other night, I was talking to someone about Tacos on Tires. Helen rushed over to interrupt the conversation. Why?"

"Because she doesn't like anyone invading her turf."

"I think that's only part of it. The entire center is gaga over Pete's tacos, which I understand, but could there be more?"

Sadie eyed her. "Like what?"

"A financial stake?"

"Most of the folks over there are on a fixed income. I doubt they'd invest in Pete since he's always a court ruling away from losing the truck."

"Then what else could it be?"

"I'm guessing you and Naomi will get to the bottom of it."

"I need to find the right chatty people and see if they'll talk," Liz said.

"Just keep Helen off your trail."

"Easier said than done."

"If she gives you a problem, threaten her with me. She and I have tangled in the past."

Liz laughed. "You constantly amaze me."

"I've been around a long time, honey."

"Then if I need to bring in the big guns, I'll let you know."

Sadie nodded. "So, were you busy while I was gone?"

"Nope. Quiet this afternoon."

"We were hopping earlier."

"By the way, where's the fabric for the Christmas stockings?" Liz asked. "I need to get started on my share and thought I'd get some stitching time in when I visit with my guests."

"I put it away until we were ready to pass it out."

"Can I get mine now?"

"Of course." Sadie walked to the storage closet.

"First, let me tell Sarah she can leave."

"Then I can tell you about poor Renee. I'm worried about her. She hasn't been this despondent since her folks died."

"Be right back." Liz traversed the hallway to the kitchen, her mood plummeting again. It was bad enough that Josh was still missing. She hated to think what this newest information would do to Renee, who grew more fragile every day. And the stress would be eating away at Josh's parents too. Liz prayed Josh was alive, but she couldn't quell her growing dread that time was running out on a happy ending.

14

"Are you sure you brought enough supplies?" Liz asked the following morning as she slammed her car trunk.

"I'm always prepared," came Naomi's snappy reply. "After spending a short time with the seniors, I've discovered I need to be on my toes."

They settled into the Acura, and Liz drove off.

"I called the director at the center to ask about any food restrictions." Naomi pulled a shopping list from her purse. "Get this. No nuts. Watch the amount of shortening. Low sugar. Oh, and I love this—gluten free."

"Wouldn't it be easier to collect bark?"

"Never fear. I came up with suitable recipes to cover the dietary limitations, but it means we have to bake an assortment of goodies."

"I want the recipes with sugar, fat, and taste."

Naomi laughed. "Everything we make will be tasty."

Soon they were at the senior center, toting in bags of ingredients. Colonel Burns still manned the door. "Morning, ladies."

Liz gave a nod. "Colonel, which way to the kitchen?"

He pointed to their right. "Cut through the dining hall. Kitchen's in back." He craned his neck to peer into the bags. "Got anything with cranberries in it?"

"You bet." Naomi winked at him. "I'll leave a muffin with your name on it."

As they ventured down the hallway, a middle-aged woman with sleek black hair, dressed in a sweater and a pencil skirt, exited an office. "Naomi?"

"Yes." Naomi shook the woman's hand. "And this is my friend Liz. You must be Donita Haines."

"I am. Pleased to meet you."

Liz juggled her bags so she could shake the director's hand. "You have my admiration. This bunch is a hoot."

"We do have our moments."

Liz noticed fine lines around the woman's eyes, and she thought her taut smile appeared forced.

"Have you decided what type of event this will be?" Donita asked, clutching a clipboard close to her chest.

Like a shield?

"A baking contest," Naomi announced, taking Liz by surprise. "We'll make a variety of samples and let the folks pick their favorite."

"Thanks for the heads-up," Liz playfully muttered.

Donita directed them to a set of double doors. "They're waiting."

Liz opened the doors, and they entered a large dining room filled with the senior set. The group watched them curiously as they crossed the room on the way to the kitchen. Once they deposited the bags, Naomi and Liz returned to the dining area to greet the seniors. At the nearest table sat Betty and Curtis, along with their friends.

"Here's the plan. Liz and I are going to bake four different types of muffins. If you break up into groups, we'll give you all a taste so you can judge your favorite."

"Good luck getting us to agree," Betty said.

"Don't listen to her," Curtis said. "We're happy to have decent food."

"Trust me, Naomi's baking is beyond decent," Liz assured them.

"What's the prize?" Curtis asked.

"One breakfast at the Olde Mansion Inn or your choice of a goody from Sweet Everything, depending on which one of us wins."

Curtis rubbed his hands together. "Now you're talking."

Donita, still gripping her clipboard, joined Liz and Naomi. "Coffee has been made. Since it will take a while for the baked goods to be ready, I've gathered some board games to play while you wait."

As the director supervised the activity, Liz thought she heard

Curtis say, "Ante up, my friends. How much are we wagering today?" But when she looked at him he portrayed the picture of innocence.

"We'd better get working fast," she told Naomi as she entered the kitchen. "If I heard correctly, Curtis is about to wrangle money out of his game mates."

Naomi removed flour and other baking supplies from the bags. "Do you think we'll be like them when we're older? Full of life and humor?"

Liz grinned. "I certainly hope so."

"I think I'm going to make the senior center a project of mine. They need company. I'd like to create a proposal to include kids from the high school. A friend-mentor kind of program."

"Sounds like you've given this serious thought."

"I was involved in a similar type of program when my grandmother was in a nursing home. I guess I have a soft spot for the elderly. Especially for Curtis."

"Who doesn't?" Liz said, laughing.

"Here are your recipe cards with the restrictions included." Naomi handed her two neatly printed cards. "I gave you pumpkin and orange-cranberry muffins. I'm taking apple-cinnamon and coffee cake."

"My stomach is growling already."

The two went to work, measuring, stirring, and getting the batter ready. Soon the pans were tucked inside the oven. While they cleaned up, Liz looked around for extra dish towels. She opened a few drawers with no success. "Did you see a storage closet around here?"

Naomi stood at the sink and glanced over her shoulder. "Try that door on the opposite wall. It must be a closet or utility room."

Liz tossed the wet towel on the counter before heading to the closet. She'd just reached for the knob when Helen barged into the kitchen.

"And what do you think you're doing?"

Liz froze. "Looking for cleaning supplies."

Helen stomped past a wide-eyed Naomi to yank open a drawer

on the far side of the sink. "Towels." She pointed to the cabinet below. "Cleaning supplies. Everything you need is right here."

"Thanks?" Liz posed it as a question because she wasn't sure if the woman was truly being helpful or super controlling.

"All you have to do is ask," Helen said, her tone softening. "We can assist you with anything you need."

Liz took the clean, dry cloth Helen held out to her. As she went back to drying bowls and utensils, she noticed one of Helen's posse standing by the closet door. The woman smiled and nonchalantly leaned against the wall. Was she camped out to keep an eye on them?

"My friends and I know the lay of the land," Helen said. "We'll hang around until you're done."

Liz raised a brow. From barking orders to helpfulness? She had mental whiplash keeping up with Helen.

Before long the scent of baking muffins wafted from the kitchen to the dining room. The group continued playing board games and conversing loudly while waiting to sample Naomi's recipes.

Once they finished cleaning up, Liz took a seat beside Betty. "I promise these muffins will be better than the cookies at the bank."

"Fresh for sure. The bank must think because we're old our taste buds don't work. I'm here to tell you they do."

"Besides the taco truck, do you have any other food services stop here?"

"Used to have folks from the sandwich shop drop by once or twice a month, but they stopped. Before that, there was a culinary school, but it closed down."

"Who cooks for the center now?"

"Mutt Phelps." Betty grimaced. "He's okay, but we like variety. He gives us the same old food."

Curtis pulled up a chair beside Liz. "And Mutt doesn't bake."

Betty crossed her arms over her chest. "We do that ourselves."

"Really? Why didn't you say something? Naomi and I could have chosen a different activity."

"Because we don't eat what we bake," Curtis said. "We sell it."

"Come again?"

Betty shot a glance at Helen who was seated a few tables away, then lowered her voice to a loud whisper. "We've been holding bake sales."

Alarm seized Liz. "Does the center need money?"

Curtis shook his head. "From time to time we raise funds for different projects. Like when we bought a sixty-inch television for the dayroom."

"Or the time we purchased new books for our library," Betty added.

"And don't forget about the karaoke machine," another woman chimed in. "That was not on the list of approved purchases."

"Stupid committee," Curtis groused.

"I think it's great that you work together." Liz applauded the group. The folks exchanged dubious glances.

"You don't work together?"

Betty sighed. "We try, but usually it's one group against another."

"So the bake sales?"

"Not our group's call this time," Betty informed her. "We pick our battles."

"Do you even know what your money will be buying?"

Betty frowned. "Helen swears we'll be happy. She's not usually this secretive, but the current project has her in a good mood so we don't argue."

What Liz had experienced was Helen's *good* mood? "I see."

The oven timer chimed.

Curtis jumped up. "Get in there, ladies. We're ready to judge."

Liz and Naomi donned oven mitts and went about removing the pans. The muffin tops had baked to a golden brown.

"Perfect," Naomi said as she inhaled.

"We forgot to bring trays to serve the muffins on."

One of Helen's group pointed to a cabinet. Once Liz found the platters, they carefully removed the muffins, allowing a few minutes for them to set and cool. Then they carried out two platters each and waited for Donita's instructions.

When Liz studied the crowd, she noticed a clear delineation of cliques. Betty, Curtis, and their friends sat on one side of the room, Helen and her group on the other. Colonel Burns was stationed by the door, his sharp-eyed gaze taking in the entire scene.

"To keep things orderly, we will serve you." Donita placed pens and slips of paper at each table. "After eating, please write down your preference on a piece of paper."

Liz and Naomi carried the muffins, then plates to each table.

The room went nearly silent as the residents chewed, savoring muffin heaven.

"What do you think?" Naomi whispered to Liz while they waited.

"I think these folks like to eat."

Finally, the muffins were gone. Donita collected the ballots, and in a couple of minutes, she looked up from her tallying. "The winning muffin is . . . coffee cake."

Naomi squealed.

"It's not like you won an award," Liz reminded her, amused by her friend's enthusiastic response.

"Sorry. I got sucked into the drama."

Donita clapped. "Since Naomi's muffins won, you all get to stop by her bakery and claim your treat."

"That's what I'm talking about!" Curtis yelled. "Get the van ready."

Naomi pulled the director aside. "Make sure to call ahead of time so I have plenty of baked goods to go around."

"Don't worry. I will."

By now, everyone had started socializing. Except Betty, Liz noticed. Curious, she joined the older woman. "Not up to visiting today?"

"Not up to kowtowing to Helen, if you want the truth."

"Yeah, what's the story with that?"

"Remember how I told you we pick our battles? I can already tell I'm not a fan of Helen's newest plan."

"I thought you didn't know what it is."

Betty looked away.

"You do?"

"See, here's the problem," Betty said, facing her. "I honestly don't know and that concerns me."

"Really, Hummingbird?"

Betty's cheeks turned pink. "The colonel's idea. He suggested we have code names. The man never could separate himself from the military."

"What was your mission in town when I ran into you and Curtis?"

"Intel gathering."

"What kind of intel?"

"Helen told Curtis, Annie, and me to go to the bank, the coffee shop, and city hall. I went to the bank to check our balance. We don't go for that electronic stuff. We each had separate missions, and I don't know what the others were looking for. Curtis blew his part, and Annie is one of Helen's girls so she could be up to anything." She gave Liz a dry look. "As you know, the mission was aborted anyway."

"By Helen's orders?"

"Yes. Something spooked her, and she wanted us to back off. Since then, she hasn't given any more instructions, but I still think she's up to no good."

"Are you sure this isn't about the taco truck? Pete said he has a new sponsor."

"If it is, it's news to me."

Liz thought about it for a long moment.

"I'm available," Betty said, breaking her concentration.

"Pardon?"

"To find out what's going on and report back to you."

"Why I . . ." Liz paused. "That's actually a good idea."

Betty grinned. "Thought you might see it my way."

"You know my main goal is to find any leads I can about Josh. Naturally, Chief Houghton is doing the official investigation, but if you hear anything interesting, please call me. We can decide if it has any merit and pass it on to the police."

"I know you want to find Josh," Betty said, "but I'm afraid we're going to let you down. Josh never visited here, and even though we support Pete and his truck competitions, Josh's disappearance has nothing to do with the senior center. No matter how much you want it to."

Liz sighed. "It's hard sitting on the sidelines, watching Renee's spirits sink more and more every day. I want to do something constructive."

"Grasping at straws is not it."

"Maybe," Liz said. Betty might not see a pattern, but she did. She just needed more time to figure it out. "I should help Naomi clean up. Call the inn if you learn anything, Hummingbird."

Betty stomped her cane. "You betcha."

When Liz returned to the kitchen, Naomi was up to her elbows in soapsuds. One of Helen's gang dried the dishes while another put the bowls and utensils away.

"Looks like you have plenty of help."

"I do. These women graciously volunteered to work with me."

Or were ordered to, Liz thought as she packed up the leftover baking supplies.

Helen waltzed into the kitchen. "We want to thank you both for baking for us. We don't get many visitors, so we appreciate it when busy folks take time out of their day to spend it with us."

What had happened to the drill-sergeant attitude? Still, Liz's heart softened again. She hated the idea that the seniors didn't get much company.

"We'd love to do it again," Naomi said as she dried her hands.

"Why don't you think of another activity we can do for you?" Liz suggested. "Maybe we can get more of our friends to participate."

"We don't need a whole bunch. You two are enough," Helen said.

Liz exchanged an amused glance with Naomi. So much for a magnanimous change. "Just let us know."

"We will. You should be going now." Helen picked up the bags and handed them to Liz and Naomi, shuffling them out of the kitchen. How many mixed signals was this woman going to send them?

The folks still in the dining room offered their thanks and invited Liz and Naomi back again.

At the door, the colonel rose. "Find what you were looking for?"

Liz stared at him. Had she been that obvious?

"Don't stop till you do," he encouraged.

"I . . . um . . ."

"I hope we'll see you soon," Naomi said, covering for her.

He saluted. "I'm sure of it."

As they walked to the car, Liz realized that in all the busyness she hadn't had a chance to poke around the center for anything out of the ordinary. They'd have to return as soon as possible because one thing was certain: Helen was hiding something.

And Liz was determined to find out what it was.

15

Late Wednesday morning Liz carried a basket of freshly laundered linens through the main floor hallway of the inn. Breakfast time had ended, and the two couples had checked out early, giving her a head start on cleaning the rooms for her upcoming guests.

Mary Ann bustled through the front door.

Liz glanced at her tardy friend. "You're late."

"Tough morning. Renee got a call from the hotel where she and Josh were supposed to spend their honeymoon asking her if she wanted to book a new date." She shrugged off her jacket. "I'm worried about her. She isn't eating or sleeping. I try to get her out of the house, but she refuses."

"I'm guessing the police still don't have any answers."

"No. And since they found the blood in Josh's car . . ." Mary Ann shivered.

"What if I call Renee and ask her to meet me for lunch? I could use our Christmas project as an excuse."

"You know, she might listen to you. I think she's starting to resent my hovering."

"I'll call her a little later," Liz said. "I have a few chores to take care of before my guests check in tomorrow."

"I can assure you she's at home. On the couch. Staring at her phone."

"Then I'd better get moving."

Liz decided to call Renee before changing the sheets. She answered on the first ring, her voice going flat when she learned it was Liz.

"I have questions about your class project," Liz said. "Can we meet for lunch?"

"You could come here."

"I could, but I'd rather go out."

"No, I'm not in the mood."

"Coffee?"

Renee hesitated.

"It'll be a short visit."

"Okay. How about one o'clock?"

"Perfect. The Coffee Cup?"

"Yes. See you then."

Liz finished her task and went downstairs to Sew Welcome. "Mission accomplished. I'm meeting Renee for coffee later."

Mary Ann looked up from the cutting table. "I'm glad she agreed."

"I thought about asking her to work on the project here, but then it occurred to me that she might not like coming back to the scene of her biggest nightmare."

"And seeing Elyse hanging around might add to her heartache."

"Any suggestions on what I should talk about?"

"Keep to the project. Renee has to report back to school next week. Before she knows it, it'll be time for her students to focus on the class project. Whether she likes it or not, she needs to be ready."

Liz snapped her fingers. "I'll bring her the stockings I've already stitched. Maybe that'll get her excited."

"Or if not excited, perhaps motivated. And while you're there, watch out for that Andrew Carter."

Sadie breezed into the shop with a cup of tea. "Andrew Carter?" She eyed Mary Ann. "What's he doing?"

"He keeps calling Renee. Sending candy and notes. It's downright creepy."

"Could that be part of the reason why she doesn't want to leave the house?" Liz asked.

"Maybe. My guess is he's pressuring her to move on so he can take Josh's place." Sadie placed her steaming cup on the sales counter. "Not very gentlemanly if you ask me."

"He doesn't seem to be able to take a hint," Mary Ann said as she folded the fabric she'd just measured and cut.

"Do we need to bring the chief in on this?" Liz questioned. "Get a restraining order?"

"Andrew's not deliberately stalking her," Mary Ann replied. "He doesn't stop by unannounced, and he calls her only once a day to check in, he says."

"Is Renee uncomfortable with his attention?"

"No, just annoyed."

"The boy can't take no for an answer," Sadie huffed.

"I'll bring it up over coffee. See if she wants the police to talk to him."

A little before one, Liz strode down Main Street. She was a few doors away from the coffee shop when Andrew walked out and headed off in the opposite direction.

Oh no. Renee.

Lengthening her stride, Liz hurried into the coffee shop. After a quick search, she found Renee at a table in the corner, dabbing her eyes with a tissue. Liz pursed her lips. She didn't like this. Not one little bit.

"Renee," she said as she reached the table and placed a comforting hand on her shoulder.

Renee sniffled and balled up the tissue.

"What's wrong?"

"It was nothing. Andrew thinks he was consoling me."

Just then Liz noticed the dozen yellow roses on the small bistro table. "It's overkill, don't you think?"

"I guess it depends on his intentions."

Liz looked at Renee. "Did he say what his intentions are?"

"He insists Josh isn't right for me. I'll get over him. That in time we'll get back together. Said he was proving it by giving me my favorite flowers." She shuddered. "No matter what I say or how many times I tell him I'll wait forever for Josh, he doesn't listen. But then, he never did."

Liz took a seat. "Mary Ann is concerned. Maybe you should tell the police."

"No. I don't want to draw their attention away from searching for Josh."

"You have to be realistic." Liz gently ran a fingertip over one of the fragrant flowers. "This could turn into a problem."

"But it hasn't. Please don't make a fuss."

Oh, she wanted to make more than a fuss, but Renee had been through enough. "For now I'll honor your wishes."

"Thank you. I can't deal with another problem. Not until Josh is found."

Liz pointed to a stack of envelopes on the table. "What's all this?"

"Since I was going to be out, I stopped by my apartment to pick up the mail."

"My goodness. That's quite a pile."

"I couldn't force myself to face real life, so I haven't been home since . . . my wedding day." Renee sighed. "I've let too much go by sitting and waiting."

"Under the circumstances, it's understandable."

Renee gestured to her mail. "I don't want to open any of it."

"Take your time."

"But I'm running out of time. I have to go back to school next week." Her eyes welled up. "How am I going to act like nothing has happened?"

"You aren't. But you'll cope. Hopefully, people will respect that."

"At least the children will get my mind off Josh. For a few hours anyway."

Liz squeezed her hand. "Don't give up." Hoping to distract Renee, she rummaged through her tote bag and removed the stockings she was using as an excuse for their meeting. "Is this what you had in mind?"

"They're beautiful." Renee studied one of the stockings. "I haven't had the energy to start on mine."

"Christmas will be here before we know it."

"I have a list of ideas for stuffers," Renee said, searching her purse.

"While you look, I'm going to order a latte." Liz wound through the tables to place her order. She looked outside to the busy sidewalk. Life went on, no matter the heartache one might be going through. She bought her drink and returned to Renee, who had placed the list on the table.

Liz read the items. "This is great." Instead of asking for donations of candy, Renee proposed that her students collect socks, gloves, or toiletries—small yet necessary items for needy kids.

"Even though my students are young, I'm always trying to get them to think beyond themselves. Given the right motivation, it's amazing how generous little ones can be."

"All they need is a teacher like you with a big heart."

Renee's cheeks flushed. "I always see the glass half full."

"Speaking of which, do you want a refill?"

"No." Renee hesitated. "But you know what I could use?"

"Name it."

"Let's go back to the inn. Seeing your stockings has made me want to get started on my own. I need to get busy. Distract my circling thoughts."

"Excellent idea."

The two collected their belongings. As Renee scooped up her mail, a large envelope tumbled to the floor. She picked it up, surprise in her eyes.

"What's wrong?"

"This feels funny." She dropped the other envelopes on the table and ripped open the larger one. As she peered inside, the color drained from her face.

"Renee?"

She turned the envelope upside down. A black leather wallet fell to the table with a *thud*; then a piece of paper fluttered beside it.

"This is Josh's wallet," Renee gasped.

"Are you sure?"

"Oh yes. I recognize it." She reached out to pick it up.

"Don't touch anything." Liz dug for her cell phone in her purse. "We should call the police."

"But it's Josh's."

"Please wait."

Renee twisted her fingers together, betraying the restraint it took to keep from holding Josh's possession.

Liz got through to the station, asking for an officer to come right over.

"Maybe there's something else." Renee gathered the stack of mail and rifled through it. She read, then tossed one envelope after another onto the table.

Liz recognized bills, junk mail, and a few greeting cards, but nothing jumped out as unusual.

Ten excruciating minutes later, Officer Gerst strode in. He scanned the items on the table. "These came in the mail?"

"Yes. I went by the mailbox at my apartment building."

He put on a pair of gloves and lifted the wallet. Looked inside. "It contains Josh's driver's license." He placed it in the plastic evidence bag he'd brought with him.

"The letter?" Renee asked.

The officer unfolded the paper and read. "Josh is okay."

"He's okay," Renee whispered as she scooted forward in her chair. "That's all it says?"

"I'm afraid so."

Renee grabbed the envelope. When Officer Gerst reached out to take it from her, she snatched it away. "I've already touched it, along with a bunch of other people." Flipping the envelope over, she scanned the front. "It's postmarked five days ago." She looked stricken. "Five days and I didn't know Josh was okay."

"How could you?"

"I should have checked the mail sooner." Renee held up the envelope. "It might have been helpful before now."

"What's that smudge on the corner?" Liz asked.

Officer Gerst gently took the envelope from Renee. "Looks like a grease smudge."

"Grease? Odd."

The officer secured the envelope in the evidence bag with the wallet. "We'll get forensics on this right away."

Renee placed a hand on his arm before he could leave. "After you've done everything you need to, can I have the wallet back?"

"I'll let you know." He folded the top of the bag and left the coffee shop.

Renee rose. "Why would someone send me Josh's wallet?"

Why indeed? And what about the grease mark? Liz's first thought was Pete, but to be honest, what were the odds of him leaving the mark? It could have come from anywhere. Yes, he claimed not knowing anything about Josh, but could he be lying? Covering up? If he did know, why send a letter that could possibly incriminate him?

Renee ran trembling fingers over her temple. "This is all so confusing. Why taunt me this way?"

An image of Andrew popped into Liz's mind. Could this be his sick way of getting Renee to rely on him? From what Liz had heard, that would not be out of character for him.

"I need to tell the Conrads." Renee retrieved her cell phone from her pocket and made the call.

As Renee relayed the latest development to Josh's parents, ideas kept circling in Liz's mind. Pete. Andrew. Both had reason to want Josh out of the picture. And apparently someone was willing to go to great lengths to keep him hidden.

Renee hung up. "They can't believe it. The judge is on his way to the police station."

"What do you want to do now?"

"Let's go back to Sew Welcome like we planned. I need to let Mary Ann know about the wallet."

They went to the inn with haste. As soon as they walked into the shop, Mary Ann and Sadie looked up from their work.

"I'm surprised to see you both here," Mary Ann said, pleasure lighting her features.

"Josh's wallet was delivered to me in the mail," Renee blurted.

Mary Ann dropped the scissors she'd been holding.

"The police have everything." Liz explained about the note accompanying the wallet.

Renee paced the shop. "All this waiting is driving me crazy. Josh is out there somewhere, and we have to find him."

"We need to be patient," Mary Ann warned.

"I'm tired of being patient." Renee stomped to the door.

"Renee," Mary Ann called out, "where are you going?"

"To the police station to demand answers."

"But—"

Sadie stepped in front of Mary Ann. "Let her go. She needs to take action."

"I should go with her."

"No. She needs to do it by herself. She's felt totally helpless up to this point. Going to the station will make her feel useful."

"Sadie has a point," Liz said. "Let Renee handle this on her own."

"I see the wisdom in your advice," Mary Ann said, brushing a hand through her ruffled bob. "But it's torture letting her go through this alone. She's like my daughter, and I want to protect her."

"A smart parent knows when to step aside," Sadie said quietly. "No matter how much it hurts."

Mary Ann let out a sigh. "When is this going to end?"

The question hung heavy over the room.

"There is one thing we're overlooking here," Liz said.

Mary Ann arched a brow. "What?"

"The letter said Josh is okay. Which means he's holed up somewhere. Now all we have to do is figure out where and find him before it's too late."

16

Later that afternoon the chief called, requesting Liz stop by the station so he could get her statement. He sounded distracted and stressed the importance of gathering all the facts. She had only about an hour to spare, so she asked Sarah to take charge of the inn while she was gone.

An unappealing gray had spread through the afternoon sky as the wind picked up. The temperature had dropped a few degrees since the morning.

Liz put on a warm jacket to fight off the chill, and with keys in hand, she slipped into her car. After placing the key in the ignition, she blew on her hands and rubbed them together, then turned the key.

Nothing.

She tried again.

Still nothing.

"Are you kidding me?" Sighing, she climbed from the vehicle and dashed to the porch for protection from the cutting wind. Pulling her cell phone from her pocket, she tapped the programmed number for Jake's Automotive Repair.

"Jake, it's Liz Eckardt. My car won't start. Any chance you can send one of your guys to the inn to check it out?"

He had a technician free and assured her he'd be there soon. Liz ducked into Sew Welcome to wait.

"I thought you were leaving," Sadie said.

Liz crossed the room to the window to keep an eye on the parking lot. "My car won't start. Jake is sending a mechanic over."

"Well, that's annoying."

Liz silently agreed, her patience running thin.

Customers perused the shop, and Sadie's steady chatter soothed her nerves as she continued to wait.

About ten minutes later a van with *Jake's Automotive Repair* painted on the side turned into the inn's parking lot.

"Help is here. I'll see you later." With an absentminded wave, Liz darted outside.

"Hey, Ms. Eckardt."

"Jake Jr., I see your dad sent the best."

The young man's face colored. "What's going on?"

"The car won't start."

"That should be easy enough to fix." He lugged a laptop from the van. "Can you pop the hood?"

She did as he requested, and soon Jake Jr. was poking around the engine, checking wires and tapping on . . . stuff.

"Battery is hooked up properly. I'll run a diagnostic." He connected the computer and intently watched the screen. "Huh."

"Is that a good or a bad huh?"

"The PCM shows no activity."

"I don't speak car. Can you translate that into layman's terms?"

"You aren't getting any power."

"Can you figure out why?"

Jake Jr. grinned. "That's what I do." He fiddled around again, prying open a compartment foreign to Liz. "Now that's odd."

"What?"

"Your fuses are gone."

A shiver that had nothing to do with the inclement weather crept over her. "I'm guessing that's not normal."

"No. Whoever messed with this had to have known what they were doing when they removed them." He glanced at her. "Has anyone worked on your car lately?"

Liz shook her head. She didn't think this car trouble was a

coincidence. Apparently, she'd rattled someone during her search for Josh. "Can you fix it?"

"Yep. Let me run back to the shop and see if we have the fuses for your model."

"Listen, I have an appointment. Go ahead and replace the parts, and I'll settle up with your dad later."

"Got it." Jake Jr. turned to leave, then stopped. "Need a ride?"

Since the weather was downright uninviting, she jumped on his offer. "Thanks. You can take me to the police station."

He raised his brows.

"Long story."

Jake Jr. dropped her off, and she entered the warm building.

Chief Houghton was standing behind a desk reading a computer screen. He looked up when Liz said hello. "Thanks for coming down. I wanted your take on Renee finding the wallet."

"I can't imagine it's much different from what she told you."

"Come with me."

She followed him to his office, where he pulled out a chair for her.

"This was the first time Renee had picked up her mail?" the chief asked as he took a seat behind his desk.

"Yes. She's still staying with Mary Ann, and she hasn't been to her apartment since the day of the wedding. Or the . . ."

"I get it." He appeared concerned. "Renee insists that Pete be brought in for questioning."

"Why?"

"Because of the grease smear on the envelope."

"That could have come from anywhere."

"But you've been questioning Pete. And you found Josh's car on his property. It's not a leap for her to connect the two."

"To be fair, I thought of Pete immediately when I saw the smear. And now . . ."

"Now?"

Liz explained what had happened to her car.

The chief's eyes went dark. "I'll send Officer Gerst over to see if he can get any prints."

"Thanks."

"You know you could have led with this information."

"Sorry. I'm still processing the idea that someone deliberately tampered with my car."

He shot her a dry look. "I'm assuming you suspect Pete?"

"He does know his way around a car."

"He's not a mechanic by trade."

"No," Liz said. "But his name has come up quite often since Josh went missing."

"I'll also ask Gerst to talk to him."

"He won't like it, especially since he was questioned after Josh's car was found on his property."

"But why target your car?"

"Why the judge's car, for that matter?" she countered.

"At least meddling with the judge's car makes sense."

"I don't think Pete runs on much sense. He seems more driven by emotion."

"Still, he's an obvious suspect. We'll know more after Gerst speaks to him." The chief leaned back in his chair. "For now, I'd like to keep this from Renee."

The tension in the room suddenly felt tangible. Liz wasn't sure how to respond.

"I don't want you putting ideas in her head. If she starts questioning our every move, it won't help her. Or us. She needs to let us work the case."

"Is that why you called me down here? To tell me to keep Renee in the dark?"

"Let me make this clear. My department is investigating. Not you. I don't want Renee to overwhelm us with demands, and I can't allow her to confront Pete. Are we understood?"

"You know I'm only trying to help."

The chief paused, as if choosing his words carefully. "I understand your concern, but your conjecture isn't helping this department or Renee."

She nodded. "I'll be more judicious."

"After your car trouble? I doubt it. Look, I'd appreciate you staying out of police business. Let me do my job. I'll handle Renee and the Conrads." The strain on his face was more noticeable than usual. He couldn't be happy with the poor progress his department had made in finding Josh.

"I hear you loud and clear."

"Thank you."

Liz left the building and began walking home. So the chief was under pressure. From the judge? Probably. She could see how a hysterical fiancée didn't help matters. But they had a lead via the grease stain on the envelope and now her stranded car. Pete. Who else in the picture had the skills to disable her vehicle? Still, the why of it niggled at her. As much as she wanted to question Pete, she was pretty sure he'd cry innocent and blame others, his usual response when pressed. She wouldn't make any headway by confronting him. All she could do was go back to the inn and take care of her guests.

Liz was so preoccupied that she nearly missed Jackson standing beside his work truck and talking to Andrew. She slowed her steps. The two spoke intently. Finally, they shook hands, and Andrew crossed Main Street, smiling.

Jackson had his cell phone in hand, intent on the screen as she approached him.

"Shouldn't the mayor be in his office doing something official?"

He grinned at her. "He should, but he's all officialed out."

"Is *officialed* a word?"

"No, but in this case it fits." Jackson dropped his phone into his pocket. "What brings you this way?"

"I had to go to the police station."

"At the risk of sounding like a broken record, I have to ask. Is something wrong?"

Liz chuckled. "That's always your first question with me."

"Because it's usually appropriate."

"This time I was there by request of the chief. He had more questions."

"Did something new come up concerning Josh?"

Liz told him about the wallet and the note.

"He's alive."

"It seems so."

The unspoken words *until he is found* hung between them.

She debated telling Jackson about her car, then thought better of it. He'd only worry. "Are you and Andrew Carter friends?"

"Not exactly. I met with the VP of the company Andrew's trying to secure the loan for. He's excited to move the operation to Pleasant Creek. As mayor, I'm happy about new job opportunities for our town. It's a win-win situation."

"So it's a done deal?"

Jackson shrugged. "Andrew seems to think it is. He sent the applications to the underwriter, and now we wait."

"Did he ever mention if this was the same company he and Josh were both vying for?"

"He never came right out and said it, but I assume it's the same one."

"I guess Josh's disappearance works to his advantage."

"You really think Andrew could be responsible for Josh going missing? It seems like a stretch to me."

"The company Andrew works for is legit, right?" Liz asked.

"As far as I know. I've never heard otherwise."

"Okay, then let me ask you this. Did Andrew mention Renee when you spoke?"

"Only that he was upset about what she'd gone through and wanted to be available in case she needed him."

"Hmm." Liz smirked. "I suppose that includes phone calls, flowers, and hinting they might get back together?"

Jackson shoved his hands into his pants pockets. "Unfortunately, that sounds like Andrew's MO."

"I suggested to Renee that she tell the chief about his uninvited attention."

"By the look on your face, I take it you didn't like her answer."

"She's overwhelmed, and this thing with Andrew is at the bottom of her list. So instead, the Material Girls are keeping tabs on him."

"I'd hate to be in his shoes."

Liz lifted her chin. "If he hasn't done anything, he has nothing to worry about."

"And if he has?"

"Then we sic Mary Ann on him."

"Now I'm downright scared."

They laughed.

The sky suddenly turned gloomier, and Liz felt a couple of raindrops. "I need to get going. See you later." She waved to Jackson as she hurried down the sidewalk, hoping to make it home before the rain hit.

Once inside the inn, she shivered with relief. She found Sarah and sent her home, spent a few quality minutes petting Beans, who barely lifted his head from his favorite rug, then went to Sew Welcome to tell her friends the police chief had warned her off Josh's case. To her surprise, Judge Conrad stood by the counter, deep in discussion with Mary Ann.

Sadie sidled up to Liz. "He's been here for thirty minutes."

"Why?"

"He claims he's concerned about Renee, but he asked if you were home."

"Not the judge too."

Sadie sent her a sharp look.

"Never mind. I guess I should see what he wants."

She straightened her shoulders and greeted the judge. "I understand you wanted to see me?"

"Yes. May we speak in private?"

"Certainly. Let's go to the four-season room." As they passed through the kitchen she asked, "Would you like some coffee?"

"No thanks. I've had enough for one day."

They took seats facing each other in the empty room.

The judge broke the silence. "I wanted to thank you for finding Josh's car."

"Unfortunately, it didn't give us any clues to his whereabouts."

"No, but it put Pete back on my radar. Did you know he paid off his fines?"

"He said he was going to."

"Do you know where he got the money?"

"No. Only that he has a sponsor."

The judge frowned. "This newfound cash infusion has me concerned."

"Do you think it has anything to do with Josh?"

"I don't know how. The bank would never lend Pete any more money, and anyone who knows Pete would be foolish to just hand over cash to him."

"Yet somehow he found a way."

"I remembered you saying Josh was upset over a phone call the night of the rehearsal dinner. What did he say again?"

Liz thought back. "He told whomever was on the other end to do what needed to be done."

"So it has me thinking. Was Josh indirectly involved with Pete's money? Maybe he knew about the cash infusion and tried to stop it. That would explain why Pete would be angry with him."

"Pete only complained about the delinquent loan payments."

"True. But in court he made it clear that he'd find a way to get back at me, without blatantly threatening me."

Liz nodded. "Your brakes."

"Exactly."

"Perhaps it was meant to be a warning and had nothing to do with Josh."

They sat in silence for a moment.

Liz wrestled with whether or not to inform the judge about her car and decided against it. Instead, she asked, "Are you concerned Pete might try to physically hurt you? I mean, no one has proved he sabotaged your brakes, even if it seems likely."

"At this point I don't know what to think. I've warned Elyse to be aware of her surroundings when she goes out, and the chief assigned a patrol car to pass our house regularly."

"On the flip side, since Pete came into money, you'd think that would be enough to get him to back off," Liz mused.

The judge's lips curved into a slight smile. "Pete has a complex. He thinks everyone is out to get him. I doubt he'll back off until he's made a point."

Like tampering with my car? "You seem pretty sure."

"You must remember your years as an attorney. Over time you begin to recognize the true nature of people. Trust me, Pete will mess up again. He always does."

"And when he does, you'll be the presiding judge, and this will all go back to square one."

"My concerns exactly." The judge stood. "Thank you for your time. I wanted to hear from you what my son said that night."

"I wish I could do more."

"You ladies have welcomed Elyse into your fold, and for that I can't thank you enough. And as for Renee, it will take more than time to heal her heart."

"Like Josh coming home."

The anguish in his eyes made her chest ache.

"And what about you?" Liz asked.

"I'll keep looking over old cases. Stay in touch with Chief Houghton.

Unless the police have solid proof that a particular person cut my brake lines, I'm at a standstill."

The same was true for her car. She suspected Pete, but what if the perpetrator was another person entirely?

17

Thursday morning after retrieving the mail, Liz passed Sew Welcome and heard Sadie calling her name. She turned on her heel and picked up her pace to the shop.

She entered to find Sadie and Mary Ann behind the counter, staring at the computer screen. "Do you need me?"

Sadie beckoned her over. "Remember how I got my new phone right before the rehearsal dinner?"

"Yes. You said you had no idea how to use it, but you were excited anyway."

"I mainly wanted it for the camera. I love to take pictures of our students' work when they take a class here."

"So . . . ?"

"I needed practice, and I snapped a bunch of shots at the rehearsal party. With everything going on, I just now learned how to download them to the computer."

Liz assumed there was a point to this conversation, so she crossed the room to stand beside the other women. Sadie had a slide show of her pictures running. "What am I looking at?"

"Wait. Let me figure out how to stop this."

Liz took over the mouse, made a few clicks, and the pictures stopped moving.

"Now, let me get to . . ." Sadie's voice trailed off as she clicked through the photos, finally stopping on a fuzzy shot of people dancing.

Liz squinted. "Why is this blurry?"

"I was boogying while I took the pictures, but that's not important." Sadie motioned to the screen. "Look closer."

"I'm sorry. All I see is a group of people having a good time."

"Here." Sadie pointed to the left side of the picture.

Liz noticed a solitary figure in the shadows. "Who is it?"

"That's what I wondered, so I checked the other pictures." Sadie clicked again. Two more photos of the stranger. "Then I found this shot."

The final picture came into view. It showed Renee and Josh, his arm around her, both of them laughing. A lone figure stood off to the side in partial darkness. Now Liz could make out the shape as a man. When she leaned in to get a better look, she blinked in disbelief. "Andrew?"

"Yes. I think he must have been watching the entire party that night. With such a lively group of guests, no one noticed."

"He certainly wasn't invited," Mary Ann fumed. "Nor would he have been welcome."

A chill skittered down Liz's spine. "We need to warn Renee."

———————————————————

Later that afternoon, the Material Girls camped out in Mary Ann's living room for an emergency meeting.

Renee had been shocked to learn about the discovery on Sadie's pictures. "I didn't even know Andrew was on the property that night."

Sadie nodded. "From the way he stayed in the shadows, it's obvious he didn't want anyone noticing him."

The young woman shivered. "We hadn't spoken in a long time. I had no idea he was still interested in me."

"More like obsessed," Caitlyn mumbled.

Opal swatted Caitlyn's leg. "We don't know for sure."

"You're sticking up for him?"

"Not at all. My point is that if he was stalking Renee, wouldn't he have shown his true colors before the wedding?"

"The wedding was probably the catalyst," Liz reasoned.

"So he does something to Josh, and I'm supposed to fall into his arms?" Renee's face flushed. "He's crazy!"

"Maybe," Sadie said, "but we don't know why he was there. While the pictures tell one story, he might have an explanation."

"Like what?" Naomi asked.

"Perhaps he wanted to make sure Renee was truly happy. Assure himself that Josh was taking care of her."

"It's kind of late." Caitlyn scoffed. "They broke up. Renee moved on."

"I did."

"You all are going to make me say this, aren't you?" Mary Ann took a deep breath. "We have to confront him. Ask him to explain."

Liz remembered Chief Houghton's warning. "We should let the police handle the matter."

Everyone looked at Liz.

She threw her hands up. "What?"

"From the beginning, Renee asked us to investigate," Mary Ann reminded her.

"That's very true, but the chief warned me not to stick my nose into their investigation."

"Do we know for sure they're investigating Andrew?" Sadie asked.

"No."

"Then we aren't impeding their process."

"And besides," Naomi teased, "since when do you get scared off?"

"I'm not scared," Liz said, "but I can't think of any other ways to find Josh."

The room went silent for a drawn-out moment.

"Any ideas going forward?" Sadie pressed the group.

This time the women looked at Renee.

"I don't care if any of you talk to Andrew, but from now on, I'm not answering his calls or opening the door if he stops by. He might not know anything about Josh vanishing, but the fact that he was at the rehearsal dinner is too disturbing to contemplate."

"Liz," Mary Ann said, "are you still going to abide by the chief's warning?"

"C'mon, you know me better than that." Liz paused for a moment, an idea stirring in her head. "We could track Andrew down and demand answers, but to what end? He won't say a word if he knows where Josh is and that we're on to him. For now, we observe." She turned to Renee. "I agree with you that it's better not to interact with him. Until we know for sure what he's up to."

"How do we find out what he's up to?"

"I think he must meet with clients at The Coffee Cup because I've seen him there at different hours of the day. We can take turns checking his office and the coffee shop."

"How will we know if he's doing anything. . . out of the ordinary?" Opal asked.

"By comparing notes," Liz decided. "Right now, I believe it's our best bet."

They came up with a quick schedule. Once the meeting ended, the women talked about Renee's class project and soon went off in different directions.

Naomi stopped Liz in the driveway. "Do you have a moment to talk?"

"Sure. Sarah is handling the afternoon snack at the inn."

"I went back to the senior center today. I wanted to talk to Donita about the retirees interacting with younger people. We had a wonderful visit. It seems there are existing programs available, so we discussed which ones would work best."

"Wonderful. I know you were excited when you mentioned it."

"Yes, it's a good start, but something odd happened when I was there."

"Something odd happens every time we stop by there." Naomi seemed to consider her words. "True."

"So tell me."

"I talked to Donita about another baking contest, this time including Mary Ann's pies. She was pleased with the idea of having another activity for the seniors."

"You'll lose if you go up against Mary Ann."

"I know, but the seniors will enjoy her pies." Naomi's face grew sober. "After speaking to Donita I went to the kitchen to check out what kind of baking equipment we might be able to use. There were two women in the kitchen huddled over the counter, speaking in hushed tones. When they realized I had walked into the room, they quickly turned to face me, blocking whatever they were doing. I said hello, and they stumbled all over themselves to chat, never moving from the spot. It wasn't a minute later that Helen arrived."

"Surprise, surprise."

"She went on and on about our visit the other day and how much she enjoyed the muffins, eventually getting me to step out of the kitchen. We spoke for a while before I told her I needed to go. I peeked in the kitchen one last time before leaving, and the two women were gone. But I never saw them leave the room."

"Where could they have gone?" Liz asked.

"I tried to remember if there was an outside door leading from the kitchen, but I came up blank."

"There has to be another way."

"In light of your suspicions about the older folks, especially Helen, I thought you should know."

Liz checked her watch. "I still have time before Sarah goes home for the night. Maybe I'll swing by the senior center and do a little reconnaissance."

"Ooh, a military term. Maybe you should ask the colonel to join you."

"He definitely knows things. Unfortunately, I'm not sure what exactly I'm suspecting the seniors of doing."

"I'd go with you, but I have to get back to the bakery. I have a special order I need to prep for."

"Thanks for the heads-up." Liz strode to her repaired car, turning on the heat once she started the ignition. Late afternoon cloud cover created shadows even before dusk fell, and the wind had picked up again.

She sat for a moment, her mind whirling. The seniors. Andrew. Pete. There was no way they could all have connections to Josh's disappearance. Pete had a sponsor and a new influx of money, but the seniors had no beef with Josh. Which left Andrew, who still had a thing for Renee. But doing something to get Josh out of the way? Wasn't that too obvious?

Out of answers, Liz backed out of the driveway and drove to the senior center. If anything, running into Betty, Curtis, and Colonel Burns would cheer her up.

She was just about to enter the parking lot when a compact car cut her off and zoomed in front of her. She slowed, then idled, waiting. The car whipped into the closest space, and the door flew open. Andrew emerged.

Surprised, Liz pulled into the nearest spot, not wanting to call attention to herself. She parked and turned off the engine, her gaze following Andrew as his long strides ate up the sidewalk. He went inside, and through the glass, Liz could barely make out another figure. She squinted, but from this distance, she didn't recognize the hazy shape. They spoke for a few minutes before moving farther into the center.

"Finally," Liz huffed. As much as she'd itched to get out of the car, she didn't want Andrew to see her. Thankful for the chilly day keeping most people indoors, she jogged up the sidewalk. Once at the door, she peered inside. There was no one visible.

Quietly, she opened the door and slipped into the building. For a usually hopping place, it was eerily silent. She decided to check the dining room. Her first steps seemed to echo in the hallway, so she tread lightly.

At the entrance to the dining room, she peeked inside. Empty. It was nearly time for supper. *Why isn't anyone here?* Just as well. Now she could examine the kitchen without being discovered.

Rushing across the dimly lit room, Liz stumbled into the dark kitchen. She hated to turn on the overhead lights, but she would never see anything out of the ordinary in the shadows. She flipped on the lights.

The room was as clean and tidy as the day she and Naomi had baked here. She scanned the four walls. No other door besides the closet. If Naomi hadn't seen the women leave, where had they gone?

Curious, Liz started a circuit of the room. Nothing unusual for a kitchen, except there was no cook at dinnertime. She reached the closet door and turned the knob.

Nothing.

She tugged again.

Locked.

It made sense. The management probably wanted certain things kept from the general public. Liz checked the refrigerator, which was nicely stocked. She opened all the lower cabinet doors. No one hiding inside. Then she searched the top cabinets, but each was neatly organized with either cups and plates or spices and other cooking supplies. She stood still, trying to come up with a plausible scenario for Naomi's story, when she heard voices in the hallway.

How was she going to explain her presence?

First, Liz needed to get out of the kitchen. If anyone found her snooping around, suspicions would abound, and she didn't have a handy reason for showing up unannounced.

She'd gotten halfway across the dining room when a middle-aged man with bushy hair and a droopy mustache, wearing a white chef coat and pants, walked in. He halted when he saw Liz. "Can I help you?" he asked, his voice husky.

"Hi. I came by to visit my good friend Betty. I thought she'd be at dinner"—Liz gestured to the empty room—"but no one is eating."

The man visibly relaxed. "There's a big meeting going on in the dayroom. I was involved until just now, so dinner is late getting started."

"That explains it." She smiled. "Are you the cook?"

"Yep. And I'd best get at it. A bunch of hungry folks will be coming through those doors soon." Mutt started to walk away, then stopped. "You want me to tell Betty you stopped by?"

"No thanks. I'll walk over to the dayroom and catch her myself."
He journeyed on to the kitchen.

Letting out a breath, Liz escaped down the hallway. By the front
door she paused. Should she go to the dayroom or make her getaway
now? As much as she wanted to know who Andrew was here to see,
did she risk a chance at being seen by him?

Still deciding, she heard footsteps behind her. She turned around
to see Colonel Burns marching toward her.

"Liz, to what do we owe the honor?"

"I . . . uh . . . stopped by to check out the kitchen. Naomi had
another baking idea, and I wanted to be sure we had the correct equipment."

"Kitchen's pretty well stocked."

"I noticed. All we need to bring are the ingredients."

"You really lit up the place the other day. Folks are still talking
about those muffins. Curtis has been after Donita to line up the van
for a visit to the bakery."

"Actually, I'm surprised he hasn't walked over."

The colonel grinned. "We aren't spring chickens anymore. We
might be able to walk one way, but we need a ride back."

"Then you should definitely wait for the van."

"Are you going to see Betty or Curtis while you're here?"

"I think it's getting close to dinnertime. Perhaps I should come back."

"No need. We take visitors anytime." He jerked his thumb
behind him. "Just saw that young Andrew. Did you run into him
in the kitchen?"

Liz's heartbeat picked up. "No. He was there?"

"Yes, ma'am. Passed him myself."

"Was he alone?"

"Yes, again." He glanced down the hallway. "You didn't see him?"

"No, the room was empty."

The colonel rubbed his chin. "That doesn't make sense."

"I'll be right back." Liz sprinted to the kitchen. The cook glanced at her, but she motioned for him to carry on. She checked the room again but couldn't find another exit. "Excuse me."

Mutt stopped chopping vegetables and looked her way. "You need something?"

"Was anyone in the kitchen when you came in?"

"Nope."

"Is there any other way to leave this room?"

He shook his head. "Just the door you came through."

"Thanks," she said, then returned to the main entrance.

The colonel was still there. "Any luck?"

"No, I must have missed Andrew."

"Did you need to talk to him?"

"Not really. I just thought it was odd that he might have headed to the same place, but we never crossed paths."

The colonel shrugged. "Happens around here a lot."

"Well, I need to get back to the inn."

"Should I tell anyone you were here?"

"That's okay. I'll check in with Betty later."

"You got it."

Liz had gotten no more than four steps out the front door when she stopped in her tracks. Andrew's car was gone.

18

"It's official," Liz announced as she strolled into the bakery a few minutes before closing time. "I've lost it."

"Lost what?"

"My mind."

Naomi grinned. "I don't think that's possible."

"Oh yeah? Wait until you hear the latest."

"Fine, but let me get us both a cup of coffee. Then you can regale me." Naomi filled two cups and carried them to the table where Liz had taken a seat. "Proceed."

Liz told her about following Andrew and losing sight of him.

"Wow. I understand your confusion. That's how I felt earlier today when I saw the women in the kitchen and then"—she snapped her fingers—"they were gone."

"I'd like to blame it on secret tunnels, but the building is too modern. I highly doubt Andrew was beamed anywhere, and time travel is too . . ."

"Outrageous?"

Liz snorted. "Yes. Right along with alien abductions."

"Then we can rule out the paranormal as well."

"Until I come up with concrete answers." She paused. "Although the colonel made a cryptic comment about people missing each other like that. He said it happens around the center often."

"It can't be a coincidence."

"Exactly. Because I know Andrew was there." Liz pondered her dilemma. "If I'd seen who he was talking to, it might have helped me locate him, but for now, how he got away is a mystery. I'm telling you, there's no way he could have been in the kitchen without me seeing him."

"There must be another exit we don't know about."

"There has to be. And we need to find it." Liz blew on her coffee before taking a sip.

"We?"

"Yes. You have an in at the center now. If you show up, say, to bake more muffins, no one would question you snooping around."

"And while I'm snooping what will you be doing?"

"Figuring out who Andrew went to see and why," Liz said.

"How do you intend to do that?"

"I'm not sure. Give me some time to think about it, and I'll come up with a solution."

The women drank their coffee in silence. Liz stared out the window, watching the wind whip tree branches, leaves scattering to the ground like collateral damage.

"You know," Naomi said, breaking the quiet reverie, "this Saturday will be two weeks since the wedding day. What if Josh still isn't found?"

"I don't want to think about the worst-case scenario." Liz sighed. "I can still picture the joy on his face the night of the rehearsal dinner. How he couldn't wait for Renee to open his gift before the ceremony. He was excited to be getting married and looking forward to what the future held for the two of them."

Naomi straightened her shoulders. "Tomorrow I'll go back to the center, bake up a storm, and see what I can discover in the process."

"Thanks for helping me with this."

"We promised Renee. I'm just doing my part."

"I have to say, I have the best friends in the world."

Naomi smiled. "Right back at ya."

Liz rose. "Well, this was only a quick reprieve. I have to get over to the inn and see what's been going on since I left earlier this afternoon."

Gathering their cups, Naomi frowned.

"What is it?"

"I can't decide what kind of muffins to bake tomorrow. Blueberry or banana spice?"

"You're already a hero at the center. Either one will earn high praise."

"The seniors are special."

"Yes, and they're obviously up to something."

Naomi laughed.

Liz went outside, shivering in the raging wind. There was an atmospheric change going on, and Pleasant Creek was in for bad weather. She hoped it wouldn't deter her booked guests from making the trip.

As Liz hurried into the kitchen, rubbing her chilled fingers, Sarah met her. "Your weekend guests, the family from Chicago, are running late," she said. "They expect to be here later tonight."

"Thanks for the update. Late is better than canceling."

"Also, Kiera left this for you. She waited for a while but had to go home." Sarah handed Liz a plastic bag. "She said you would want to see it."

Puzzled, Liz took the bag and opened it. She raised her brows when she saw a crumpled object inside. Not wanting to touch it, she dumped it on the counter.

Sarah stood beside her, her head cocked. "It looks like paper."

"I see words printed on it." Liz opened a cutlery drawer and removed two forks.

"What are you doing?"

"I don't want to touch it in case it has to do with Josh's disappearance." With a fork in each hand, she managed to spread the crumpled card stock flat enough to read it.

She clamped a hand over her mouth at the same time Sarah said, "My goodness."

"Renee and Josh's wedding invitation." Liz stepped back and looked at Sarah. "Did Kiera say where she found it?"

"In the parking lot."

Strange. Liz already knew that Andrew had been lurking around the rehearsal dinner. Had he gotten a hold of an invitation and wadded it into a ball in a fit of anger, then dropped it? But what about Pete? If he had cut the brake lines on the judge's car, he could have been on the premises too. Her head throbbed as she considered possible scenarios.

"I'm going to call the police. They'll need this." Liz placed the call, asking for the responding officer to enter the inn through the utility-room door. She turned to Sarah. "Why don't we keep this between ourselves for now? Hearing about the ruined invitation will only upset Renee."

"I agree." Sarah brushed her palms against her skirt. "I must also tell you something."

What else can there possibly be?

"Isaac and I spoke last night. He told me Josh confided in Caleb about a new loan he was working on. There were some problems, and that is why Josh was so troubled before the wedding. He told Caleb he could not go into detail, but he was in over his head and hoped to sort it all out soon. Then he disappeared."

"I wonder if Josh confided in anyone else."

"I do not know. But Isaac and I decided it was best someone else knew that there were problems in case Caleb's information could help Josh's case."

"I can't thank you enough for confiding in me."

"I know you are still searching for Josh."

"Yes, and as I told Naomi, we have to find him soon."

But how?

Before Liz could dwell further on the question, Sadie popped her head into the kitchen. "Emergency meeting in Sew Welcome."

"Another one?"

"Emergency," Sadie repeated, then left.

"Sarah, you can head home. And again, thank you for confiding in me. Tell Isaac I appreciate it."

"I will." She gathered her things and left by the side door as Officer Gerst came in, stomping his feet on the mat by the door.

"You called?" he asked as he entered the kitchen.

Liz led him to the counter. "One of my employees found this in the parking lot."

The officer read the invitation. His expression turned dark.

"I haven't told Renee."

"It may not be of any concern, but I'll take it back to the station."

"But it could be?"

He eyed her. "Is there a particular reason you're asking?"

Liz proceeded to tell Officer Gerst about the pictures Sadie had uncovered on her phone.

"I need to see them."

Liz's stomach dropped. "I was afraid you'd say that."

Minutes later, Liz and Officer Gerst joined the Material Girls, each one accounted for in the shop.

Renee's eyes widened when she saw him. "Is there any news?"

"No. Ms. Eckardt informed me about the pictures on Ms. Schwarzentruber's phone. I'd like to see them."

"Better yet, I can print them out," Sadie said, already on her way to the computer.

An uneasy silence descended on the room as they waited for the printer to spit out the copies.

Gerst studied them before his gaze pierced Renee's. "Did you have any idea someone was watching you?"

Renee shivered. "Are you kidding? I would have asked him to leave."

"Him?"

Renee pointed to the top copy. "That is definitely Andrew Carter."

"Once I get these back to the station we'll determine the identification of the person."

All the women spoke at once, assuring the officer that Andrew was indeed the man in the pictures.

Gerst held up his hand to stop them, then focused on Renee. "I'll get back to you on this."

"So you keep saying," she accused as he left the room.

Liz followed to make sure he collected the bag from the kitchen. "Will you talk to Andrew?"

"That's up to the chief," Officer Gerst answered, his face impassive.

"You know I'm going to follow up."

A slight grin curved his lips. "I'll be sure to inform him."

She let the officer out and returned to the shop, which was once again teeming with activity.

Renee, who had been pacing the room, hustled over to Liz. "What did he say? Will the pictures help in the investigation?"

"He didn't say much."

Renee's shoulders slumped. "This is torture."

Liz put her hands on Renee's shoulders and held her at arm's length. "Do not give up, young lady," she said with authority.

After the pep talk, Renee straightened and lifted her chin.

"Now, let's get to work." Liz glanced around the room. "What's this new emergency?"

Renee resumed her pacing. "I miscalculated the deadline for the class project since I've been so worried about Josh. Today I realized that the PTA wants the Christmas stockings handed in before the Thanksgiving break. I forgot they need a head count and to make sure they have enough stuffers to go around." She rubbed her temples, the pinched look around her eyes indicating the amount of stress she was under. "That gives us only a few more weeks to complete them."

"I told her not to panic," Sadie said as she cut fabric.

"I'm on a roll, it seems. Living in a state of panic has become natural to me now."

Mary Ann crossed the room to give her goddaughter a hug. "The stockings are the least of your worries. We're on it."

And indeed they were. Caitlyn and Opal manned two of the

sewing machines, stitching the stockings together, Naomi traced the design onto the border once they finished, and Mary Ann had started hand stitching. All Liz had to do was jump in.

"I thought everyone had their fabric at home," Liz commented, looking at the rapidly growing stack of stockings.

"Only you," Renee said. "We hadn't gotten as far as handing out the pattern and material to everyone because I thought we had more time."

Opal turned from her position at the sewing machine. "Please don't let yourself get upset. We will finish this project."

"You have enough to think about," Caitlyn called over her shoulder.

Renee wrung her hands. She looked down and folded them in her lap. "Going to the police station didn't help. I may have been a reminder that Josh is missing, but my presence didn't bring any more clues to light. Or push the investigation along."

"What does the judge have to say?"

"Nothing. He never found a connection between his cases and Josh." She started pacing again. "To top it off, Mr. Fairfield from the bank called me today. He asked me to come down and clean out Josh's desk. Why now? It hasn't even been two weeks."

For Renee, her life was at a standstill. For the rest of the world, life went on.

"Surely he hasn't hired someone to take Josh's place," Opal said, clearly outraged.

"Mr. Fairfield said that since the police can't find Josh, he has to think about the good of the bank. I don't know what he means. It isn't like Josh would have been back to work yet anyway." Renee choked back a sob. "It's almost like he doesn't think Josh will return and is making preparations to fill his position. We don't even know what's going on."

"No wonder Betty doesn't like him," Liz said to Naomi.

"I put him off. I know I'll have to get Josh's things sometime, but right now . . ."

"What kinds of things does he keep at the office?" Caitlyn asked.

"The usual. His nameplate. A signed baseball in a clear plastic display case. Specialty pens with his name and work number printed on them." Her voice broke. "A picture of me."

"I love those free pens," Sadie cut in.

Renee sniffled. "He'd just ordered them too."

Liz thought of the merchandising business that Jackson said Josh had been working with. "Through a local company?"

"No, I think he mentioned a company from out of town."

The new company that's moving to town? Had Josh been making headway on the loan before he disappeared? By all accounts, he was stressed from working on a loan. Josh had even told Caleb that he was in over his head. Maybe the pens were a show of good faith from the manufacturer.

Liz debated telling the group about her earlier conversation with Sarah. She feared doing so would only give Renee more false hope. After all, no one knew exactly what Josh had been referring to.

"Liz, Renee asked you a question."

She started. "Sorry. What did you say?"

"I wanted to know if you'd learned anything new."

Liz bit her lower lip and scanned the room. She decided to go with her gut and keep her conversation with Sarah to herself. "Nothing helpful."

"Then we keep praying," Sadie said with her usual optimism. "Josh is out there somewhere, and he will come home."

Liz chanced a look at Renee. By her dejected expression, she didn't know what to think.

"Let's get back to work." Mary Ann clapped. "I ordered to-go sandwiches, so we don't have to stop and prepare dinner."

"Great, because my stomach is growling," Caitlyn, still dressed in her hospital scrubs, told the group.

Renee responded with a weak smile, but at least she was making an effort.

Everyone got busy cutting, sewing, and stitching.

Soon a loud knock sounded on the front door. Liz answered it and helped deliver the food to the kitchen. "Thirty-minute break," she called out.

The group filed into the kitchen, filling plates to carry to the dining room. They ate quickly, with few words. Liz offered to clean up alone so the others could get back to work.

Mary Ann, the last one to linger in the kitchen, stared at Liz.

"Now what?" Liz asked.

"You've been distracted ever since you came into the shop. What's wrong?"

Liz rolled her neck back and forth. "Everything is wrong. I feel like I'm letting Renee down."

"How? By actively looking into Josh's disappearance? You can't magically produce any clues that will lead us to him. We have to work with what we have."

"Which isn't much." Liz turned on the tap and squeezed dish soap into the sink. "What if Josh is never found?"

"Why all the negativity?"

"Because I feel like I'm really close and I'm missing the obvious."

"You've done enough already. Between running the inn and helping Renee, I'm not surprised you're frustrated." Mary Ann leaned her hip against the counter. "I think you've put too much pressure on yourself. You're an inn owner, not an investigator. In the moment, I felt the best thing for Renee was to ask for help. To give her hope. Now I think it might have been a mistake."

"Has she thought about the future if Josh never comes home?" Liz asked.

"It's still too soon. Although getting back into the swing of school will relieve some of the pressure. In the meantime, we'll go on with our lives and hope new evidence comes to light."

"And if we don't succeed?"

"You've already gone above and beyond."

Which in Liz's book wasn't enough.

The remainder of the evening passed in a whirlwind of activity. Shortly after the ladies left, the skies opened, dumping a heavy rainstorm over the town. Liz waited up for the guests who finally made it to the inn at ten o'clock. They were thankful to be off the road and looked forward to settling into their room for the night. Despite the late hour, Liz gave them a quick tour of the inn, showed them to their room, and reminded them of the breakfast hours. Then she retired to her quarters, hoping for a good night's sleep.

But it never came. Not with the uneasy feeling that she held a key to Josh's disappearance and couldn't put her finger on it.

19

Liz was up at dawn, preparing an egg-and-spinach casserole, cinnamon rolls, and fresh fruit well before the first guest ventured downstairs. The comforting scent of coffee lingered in the dining room, and Liz downed two cups to keep herself from running out of steam.

The breakfast hours flew by, and as she cleaned up, she made a decision. She had to tell Chief Houghton about Josh and Caleb's conversation. Maybe this newest information, plus whatever the police had already learned, would give them more insight into the investigation.

At eleven, Liz removed her apron and poured kibble into the food bowl to let Beans know she hadn't forgotten about him. "Sarah, I have to run a quick errand. Will you get started cleaning the rooms?"

"On my way."

After stopping by her quarters to change into jeans and a sweater, Liz pulled on low boots and grabbed a jacket. The day had dawned chilly with a heavy cloud cover after the night's storm. She wished sunshine would break through the clouds and end the dreariness. Despite the less-than-ideal weather, the downtown sidewalks bustled with activity.

As Liz strode to the police station, she passed The Coffee Cup and peeked inside. No Andrew. Continuing on, she'd just reached the crosswalk when Andrew came around the corner of the last building on the block. Their gazes locked. Liz noticed the hard glint in his eyes and the tightening of his lips. Obviously, he was not overjoyed at running into her.

"Hello, Andrew."

"Ms. Eckardt."

"How are you doing today?"

He frowned, his flinty attention zeroed in on her. "Would you have any idea why the police came by my office this morning?"

Right to the point. "Me? Don't *you* know?"

"I missed them. I've been asked to stop by the station at my earliest convenience." Andrew yanked his phone from his coat pocket. "I don't have time for this. I have scheduled client meetings."

"I'm sure the police have a good reason."

He scowled at her, took a few steps away, then turned back. "What is it with you?"

"I don't know what you mean."

He narrowed his eyes. "Renee."

"Excuse me?"

"She's made it clear she doesn't want to see or talk to me. She said it has something to do with Ms. Schwarzentruber."

Renee had taken a stand. Good. "Renee is a big girl. She can make her own decisions."

"Even if they're bad?"

"That's not for you to decide."

Andrew opened his mouth, then abruptly shut it. His features softened. "She's my friend. I only want to help her."

Liz couldn't ignore the genuine distress on his angular features. He really did care about Renee. "We're all concerned about her situation. Emotions are running high. Perhaps you should give her some space for the time being."

"I suppose. If it'll help." He seemed lost in his thoughts.

Liz took the opportunity to catch him off guard. "It seems we have something in common. Besides Renee."

A muscle ticked in his jaw.

"The senior center. I noticed you when I stopped by yesterday. Do you have relatives there?"

"Oh, you must mean my weekly meeting. I help a few of the seniors with their finances."

"How wonderful of you to give your time to the community. Have you been doing it very long?"

Andrew's gaze darted down the street, then back to her. "For a while."

"Great. From what I've heard, they really want Pete to win the food competition."

"You know about that?" Suspicion laced his tone.

"Only that they've been raising money to help keep the taco truck in the running."

He jammed his hands into his pockets. Shifted back and forth. "Right. I gave them an opinion on that project."

"When the residents set their mind to something, there's no backing down. Since you've been helpful, I bet they asked you to counsel Pete on his money woes."

"Yeah, I advise him too."

"Then I imagine they're all in good hands."

"I guess. Look, I'm meeting a client. I need to run."

"See you around the senior center."

Andrew shot her a skeptical look before he turned and stalked away.

After the light changed, Liz crossed Main Street. She entered the police station to find phones ringing and officers typing away on computers. She located Chief Houghton and waved him over. "Sorry to bother you."

"I heard you wanted an update, but I didn't expect you so soon."

"I take it Officer Gerst warned you?"

The chief grinned. "C'mon to my office."

Once they both took a seat, he pulled out his notepad.

"Actually, the reason I came here today has nothing to do with Officer Gerst's visit." Liz related her conversation with Sarah.

His pen moved rapidly over the paper as he documented her dialogue.

"I didn't tell the officer yesterday because I wasn't sure it would matter. But I couldn't sleep last night. It kept nagging at me."

"You know we appreciate every detail." He tossed the notepad on his desk. "I'll add it to the pile of information that has gotten us nowhere."

Sensing the chief's frustration, Liz changed the subject. "Any leads on my car?"

"No. We didn't get any useful prints. For now, it's an additional aspect of the bigger investigation."

She hated for her situation to remain one more unanswered question, especially since her problems seemed tied to Josh. Chief Houghton was one of the most competent men she knew. The lack of progress on the case had to be eating away at him.

Liz left soon after, still unsettled. Maybe it was the gloomy weather. She couldn't shake her mood.

On the way back to the inn, she passed the bank. She stopped in her tracks when she noticed Andrew inside talking to the branch manager.

On impulse, Liz darted inside. Hoping to go unnoticed, she quickly walked to the counter holding pens and deposit slips. She took one out and pretended to write, studying the scene around her. The receptionist was on the phone, concentrating on taking a message. Customers waited in line at the teller windows. From her angle she could see Mr. Fairfield and Andrew deep in conversation, but she couldn't make out the words.

Where was Betty to eavesdrop when she needed her?

Deciding she wasn't going to learn anything, she turned to leave. As she passed Josh's dark office, she noticed a box on the desk. *Poor Renee.* It looked like someone was cleaning out the room before she had a chance to do it herself. Indignant, Liz strode into the office. Sure enough, the belongings Renee had mentioned were in the box. The girl was going to be upset that they'd started clearing his office without her.

Liz was about to leave when she spotted a stack of files on the credenza. She peered out into the lobby. There were still plenty of people around to conceal her presence. Edging closer, she read the top file. W&K Quality Merchandise and Manufacturing. Biting her lip, she glanced over her shoulder. Still clear. Flipping open the cover, Liz peeked at the top document. A cover letter to the IRS. Oh boy.

Before she could read the contents, she heard the sound of a throat being cleared behind her. Liz jumped, slapped the file shut, and spun around.

Jackson lounged against the doorjamb. "I'm thinking you'd better have a really good reason for being here."

Liz skirted the desk and joined him. "Shh. I don't want to get caught."

"It's broad daylight. Noon, in fact. Someone is bound to see you."

She pushed him out the door and into the lobby. "I know. It's just that Renee said Mr. Fairfield called and asked her to box up Josh's things, but she's not emotionally ready. I stopped in and noticed the box on his desk. Apparently, they couldn't wait."

"Which they have every right to do. It's probably not the most decent way to handle this unsettling situation, but it is the bank's decision."

"It's bad enough that Renee is barely making it through the day, but this?"

"This is a bump. Things will straighten out."

"I don't like it."

"Neither do I." Jackson's expression gentled. "You have to let it go."

"I suppose." She shook her head, drained from the emotional roller coaster. "Who would have thought almost two weeks ago that we'd be standing here having this conversation? Renee and Josh should be returning from their honeymoon and starting a new life together. Instead Renee has an uncertain future, and Josh's office is open game."

"Any luck with the senior center?"

"Not so far."

"Then let the police finish their investigation," Jackson said. "It's for the best."

"That's what everyone says."

"For a reason."

For the first time Liz noticed the deposit slip in Jackson's hand. "Sorry to keep you from your business." She waved him away. "Go on."

"And you?"

"Back to the inn."

They said their good-byes, Liz thinking she'd pushed her luck enough for one day.

To her pleasant surprise, she encountered Miriam in the foyer of the inn.

"Liz, I was going out to find you."

"Here I am."

Miriam smiled. "Do you have a moment?"

"For you, always."

Miriam led her into Sew Welcome. The store was brimming with customers. One shopper paid for her order while another waited in line. Other women lingered by the sewing machines in conversation with Sadie. Elyse Conrad sat at Miriam's treadle machine, slowly sewing fabric pieces together.

"I finished with my class," Miriam explained.

"Mrs. Conrad decided to take lessons?"

"Yes. For a beginner, she is picking up the basics quickly."

Liz wondered if Josh's mother knew about his belongings being removed from the bank. She was sure the news would upset Mrs. Conrad as much as it had Renee.

"I wanted to show you the progress Grace is making on her quilt." Miriam picked up a quilt top and unfolded it.

Immediately the cheerful colors brightened Liz's dark mood. She took it from Miriam and held it up. "My goodness. She's dedicated to finishing this project."

"Each day she has spent her free time stitching the pieces. I think even she was surprised at how swiftly it came together."

The pattern, with only four middle squares, resembled chunky blocks toddlers would play with, tumbling over each other in a messy pile. The center blocks were surrounded by a wide border, each side a different piece of fabric.

"With Keturah's and my help, we will add the batting and backing this weekend. Grace has already picked out the quilting design to stitch over the border."

"Are you still okay with me hanging the finished product here at the inn?"

"Oh yes. Grace wants to make you proud."

"She already has." Liz folded the quilt top and returned it to Miriam. "We'll have a special unveiling."

"Just let us know."

Liz said good-bye to Miriam and left the shop, more than ready to get back to inn business. She checked on Sarah, then moved on to the kitchen. With all her sleuthing, she'd fallen behind on planning her menus. She pored over her recipe books and came up with a week's worth of breakfast meals. Once finished, she reviewed the reservation book, then looked online. Three room requests. She noted the information and went to sign off, but instead she pulled up the search page. She typed in *W&K Quality Merchandise and Manufacturing*.

Several links to the business popped up. The official website contained information about the company, what they manufactured, and how to order. Liz noticed the address listed in Chicago. Two other links had the same information.

The final link was a newspaper article. She clicked on it and read through the story, surprised by the details. Apparently, the company had financial problems that were tied to mismanagement and faulty merchandise. The article concluded with the prediction that the company might go into bankruptcy. Could this be what Josh had discovered?

She was about to click on another page to search for public records when her cell phone blared beside her. Distracted, she answered, "Hello?"

"Liz, it's Hummingbird. You need to get over to the center right away."

"Betty?"

"Yes. How many other Hummingbirds do you know?"

"Good point."

"Enough chitchat. Naomi needs you here now."

At the mention of her friend, Liz said, "I'm on my way." She ended the call, then grabbed her purse and jacket and jogged to her car.

Ten minutes later, Naomi and Betty met Liz at the front door of the senior center. They each took an arm and practically dragged her toward the dining room.

"You two are freaking me out."

"With good reason." Betty's tone conveyed her urgency.

Liz glanced at Naomi.

"Some of the seniors couldn't make it to the bakery, so Donita suggested I bring the pastries and cookies here, since I didn't have time today to stop by and bake any muffins from scratch."

"That's very sweet of you, but I don't see the problem."

"We're working up to it," Betty answered. "Us old folks don't do things real fast anymore."

"The point is," Naomi continued, "Helen and her friends are acting stranger than ever. First, they wouldn't even let me into the kitchen, and then when I got in, they wouldn't leave me alone."

"Who is in the kitchen now?"

"The same ladies," Naomi replied. "They were putting together a tray of food and stopped when I walked in."

"We don't take trays to our rooms. All the folks eat in the dining room unless they're sick. And no one is sick." Betty pointed her cane across the room. "This isn't the first time they've done it. I've been watching the past few days, and this happens once in the morning and once at night."

Liz couldn't imagine what the women were doing, but it certainly sounded suspicious. "Then let's go check it out."

"I've got Curtis watching them," Betty informed Liz. "Anything wonky going on and he'll notice."

"I don't know." Naomi sounded worried. "He was the first one in line when I put out the cookies. Can he surveil and eat at the same time?"

Betty knitted her brows. "Probably not."

Just as they reached the dining room entrance, Colonel Burns met them at the doorway. "You ladies look like you're on a mission."

"We are. You'd best keep your eyes peeled," Betty instructed him.

"Did I miss the call?" He removed a walkie-talkie from his pocket and tapped on it with his knuckle. "Or is this thing dead?"

"I didn't call you. This is need to know."

"You told Curtis."

"And how did you figure that out?"

"You always confide in Curtis," the colonel grumbled.

"That's because he's not off sneaking a puff."

Liz held up her hand. "Can you two argue later?"

The seniors glared at each other before nodding.

Liz crossed the room, Naomi and Betty in tow.

Curtis stepped in their path. "Glad you could make it. These cookies are outstanding." He took a bite out of an oversize cookie.

"Curtis, you're supposed to be watching the kitchen."

"Oh, right. Let me get on it."

"It's too late," Betty fussed and pushed her way past.

When they finally made it to the kitchen, it was empty.

"No. This can't be right." Naomi turned to Liz. "I swear, there were two women in here a few minutes ago."

"Those women are sneaky," Curtis said as he took another bite of his cookie.

"Where's Helen?"

Curtis shrugged, seemingly more interested in the sweets than the events around him.

"I think the time has come to confront her," Liz said. "Whatever is going on, I bet she orchestrated it."

"Did I hear my name?" Helen sauntered into the kitchen followed by her crew.

Liz approached her. "I'm going to come straight to the point. What are you up to?"

"Up to? Whatever do you mean?"

Naomi cut in. "Every time one of us comes into the kitchen, you have your minions watching guard."

"Oh, I love that new minions movie," one of the ladies said.

Betty ignored the remark. "Why were you putting food on a tray? Who is it for?"

"First of all," Helen said slowly, apparently trying to rein in her temper, "we watch you because you're outsiders. We don't like people coming in and messing with our stuff."

Betty snorted.

"And secondly, the tray is for a function we've planned."

"No one mentioned a function."

"If you must know, we're getting ready for a big reveal." Helen shot a nasty look at Betty. "You are ruining our big news."

"What reveal?" Liz asked.

"I'm sure Betty has explained how we raise money for different causes. Well, I'm proud to announce a few days early that the money we've been raising has gone to Pete Hardy. We're his sponsors. Once he competes in Chicago, he'll be franchising his outfit. We have first dibs on the permanent location of Tacos on Tires here at the Pleasant Creek Senior Center."

A big smile lit Helen's face. But only hers. The women around her wore guilty looks.

"You took every cent of the money we saved up?" Betty asked Helen.

"Don't act surprised. You know my people raised more money than yours, so we get to decide where it goes."

"That's because you didn't keep us in the loop," Curtis piped up. "Sending us on false missions while you and your cohorts stole our share."

Helen frowned. "We didn't steal anything. With the help of my—I mean, a financial advisor, we have more than enough money to invest with Pete. Besides, when he opens his doors here, we'll make money. No more depending on the little bit the center doles out to us when we want to buy anything new. And we'll have better food than the slop they feed us now."

"And tacos whenever we want," another woman said.

Helen beamed at her audience. "And better yet, once a new company comes to town, we'll have Tacos on Tires merchandise to sell. We'll be rich!"

"Wait," Liz said. "You know about W&K Quality Merchandise and Manufacturing?"

"Yes. How do you know?" Helen's eyes rounded in surprise. "You're not going to try to steal our business, are you?"

"Of course not, but—"

The closet door on the far side of the kitchen opened. Two women emerged, one carrying a tray, the other holding keys. When they saw the group staring at them, their eyes went wide, and they fumbled to shut and lock the door behind them.

"What on earth are you hiding?" Liz sputtered.

Helen's composed face didn't reveal a clue.

Liz stormed over to the shorter of the two women. "Give me those keys."

Helen followed. "She will do no such thing."

"You got our money stashed in there?" Curtis asked.

"This is no one's concern."

Liz turned the knob, but it wouldn't give. She glanced at Betty. "Is Donita still here?"

"She may have left for the day."

"I'll go check." Naomi ran from the room.

"Oh dear. This is not supposed to happen." Helen pulled a cell phone from her pocket, punched numbers, and said, "Yes. Please come over. We have a problem."

Liz paced the length of the room, her stomach in knots. She was afraid of what, or who, they might find on the other side of the door.

Naomi returned moments later. "Donita is on her way. She doesn't have a key to the door, so she's hunting down the maintenance man."

"This is your last chance, Helen," Liz warned.

"You're making a mountain out of a molehill," she retorted.

"And that mole is about to bite you," Betty predicted.

As the chatter increased in volume, Donita rushed into the kitchen with the colonel right behind her. She held up a large ring of keys. "I don't know which one fits the door."

"Allow me." The colonel examined the door lock, then picked his way through a few keys. Finally, one fit and released the lock. "Eureka."

Liz held her breath as the colonel turned the knob and opened the door. It was pitch-black inside. The colonel swiped the wall to find the switch, and the overhead light flickered on.

The missing groom sat in the middle of the room tied to a chair.

20

"Josh!" Liz cried out, hurrying to his side. His head lolled down over his chest, his eyes shut. "Naomi, help me get this rope off him."

As Naomi struggled with the rope, Liz tried to rouse him. "Josh, can you hear me?" She patted his cheeks. "Josh, wake up."

He started. Then lifted his head, eyes fluttering open, and blinked. "Liz?" he slurred.

"What on earth happened?"

Josh looked around the room, clearly groggy. "I . . . I'm not sure."

Liz glanced over her shoulder. "Betty, call the police."

"No one is calling the police," Helen instructed, wrestling Betty for her cane and winning.

Betty leaned against the wall, defeat reflected on her face.

Naomi yanked the rope off Josh, dropping it on the floor.

Liz grabbed his arm to steady him, panicking when she discovered dried blood on the sleeve of his white shirt. "Naomi, call 911. I think he needs medical attention."

Naomi moved to leave the room but found her way blocked.

"He's fine," Helen said from beside Liz. "We've taken good care of him."

Josh blinked more steadily now, as if trying to stay awake.

"What's wrong with him?"

"Just a little bit of sleep medication."

"Are you crazy?" Liz exploded.

"Josh posed a problem, and we had to get him out of the way," Helen explained. "We would have returned him eventually."

"Eventually?" Liz stared at Helen in disbelief. All this time Josh had been alive. Held captive but alive. "You have to let us get help."

"He's fine," said a male voice.

Liz spun around. "Andrew, what are you doing here?"

"Unfortunately, you ruined our plans. We can't allow Josh to be found yet." He turned to Helen. "You couldn't contain things for a few more days?"

"We would have if this one"—she pointed to Liz—"hadn't been snooping around."

"I really didn't want to have to do this." Andrew pulled out a pistol and aimed it at Liz and Naomi. "Step away from Josh."

Liz grabbed her friend's hand, and the two moved away from Josh. He listed to his side.

"Someone retie him."

The two women who had been in the room earlier rushed forward to retie the rope around Josh.

"You've created a major obstacle to our plan," Andrew said.

"Whose plan?" Liz demanded.

"My great-nephew's and mine," Helen said, pride beaming on her face.

"Nephew," Betty gasped. "I didn't know."

"No reason you should."

"I—"

"Enough," Andrew interrupted, his voice deadly calm. "Now we have to keep these women quiet too."

Liz's stomach dropped. "Quiet?"

He gestured toward the corner of the room with the pistol and addressed the women who had attended to Josh. "Get the additional rope and tie those two together."

"Andrew, you can't hold us."

"Sure, I can."

"There's a whole room of witnesses here."

"I've got someone at the door," Andrew announced. "No one is leaving."

"Who would help him?" Naomi whispered.

"Three more days," Andrew rambled, pacing the room. He waved the gun as he moved. "The papers will be signed, and we can complete the plan."

Suddenly, it all clicked in Liz's brain. "The loan for W&K Quality Merchandise and Manufacturing?"

Andrew glared at her. "Yes. Josh was going to ruin everything. I had to stop him. Now I will stop you."

"You need to think this through."

"I did. But then you kept searching for Josh. No matter how I tried to stop you."

"But how—?"

"And then you and your friends poisoned Renee against me. I would have won her back."

"By kidnapping her fiancé?" Liz was stunned.

"She never would have known it was me."

"Once you let him go, she would have."

"Maybe I don't plan on letting him go."

Taut silence stretched over the room.

"Wait a minute, young man." Helen pointed a finger at him. "You will stick to the original plan."

"Which is completely ruined now, thanks to you."

"We agreed." Helen's voice wavered.

A dangerous glint appeared in Andrew's eyes. "I'm calling the shots here, not you."

"This was my idea," whined Helen.

"It doesn't matter. I'm taking over this operation."

"Please," Liz begged, "will someone explain what is going on?"

Andrew's eyes were bright. Manic almost. "I will sign off on the loan. Once I get management straightened out at W&K, we'll start making money. Oh, by the way, Auntie, I invested a portion of our money in the company."

"You invested our money in the merchandise company too?" Helen screeched.

Andrew ignored her. "The seniors will get control of the taco truck because, let's face it, Pete will lose their money."

"We can't run the truck without Pete," Helen insisted. "We were only supposed to solve his money woes while he did what he does best. Cook. We talked about franchising to earn our initial investment back, but investing in a new venture? You changed the game plan."

"I had a better idea," he snapped.

Liz stared at Helen. "You came up with this scheme?"

"It's not a scheme. It's a good financial plan."

"Which just fell apart," Curtis pointed out.

Helen turned on Andrew. "When were you going to tell me you invested our money in the company?"

"After the loan went through. After I turned the company around and made us more money than you could ever imagine."

"You lied to me. You were never going to let Josh go free."

"No. After all goes as planned, I'll get the girl too."

"Renee will never forgive you." Liz swallowed her revulsion. "What you did to Josh is unconscionable, let alone illegal."

Helen tried to brush the huge fact away, but she didn't look as convinced as minutes before. "It'll all work out in the end."

Josh stirred, lifting his head. "Andrew didn't tell you?" he croaked.

Helen crept toward him. "Tell me what?"

"The loan. It will never be approved. You may get Pete's cooking, but that's it."

Helen staggered back a few steps. "Andrew?"

"Pay no attention to him."

"The loan is bogus," Josh rasped before his head slumped forward again.

Helen whirled on Andrew, her face turning red. "What did you do?"

"I ignored Josh. He doesn't deserve Renee or a place in the business world."

"*What. Did. You. Do?*"

Andrew looked around wildly. He ran his free hand through his hair, leaving it in tufts. "I followed the plan."

Helen shook her head. "But Josh just said—"

"Stop. Josh is wrong."

"About what?"

Andrew paced. "About W&K. He tried to convince me they were going bankrupt. That they submitted false numbers on the loan application. But I know better. He was trying to make me look bad, like I couldn't do my job. Like he's smarter than me. He lied so Renee would never know I'm the better man."

Liz pictured the IRS file in Josh's office. So that was what he'd discovered about the merchandise company. No wonder he had been stressed.

Helen's face paled. "We agreed to keep Josh here because you promised everything would work out."

"And it still will."

"Not now. You'll be fired. Arrested." Her voice rose. "Along with us."

"No." Andrew faced his great-aunt. "We wait. We keep quiet and we win."

"Except we won't," Helen whispered, finally realizing her great-nephew had lost everything they had worked for in his vain attempt to prove his worth to Renee.

A commotion sounded in the dining room. The police burst in, along with the EMTs. In the flurry of activity, Liz noticed Chief Houghton and two of his officers had their guns drawn at Andrew, who had the good sense to lower his weapon.

"Put it on the floor!" Officer Dixon shouted.

Andrew gently deposited the pistol on the floor.

"Hands up."

Once Andrew complied, Officer Dixon rushed over, kicked the gun away, and yanked Andrew's hands behind his back to slap on handcuffs.

After speaking in urgent tones, the paramedics untied Josh. He was conscious for the few moments they shined a light in his eyes and checked his vitals. Once he was freed from the rope, they placed Josh on a gurney. He was still spacey, his head falling to one side and then the other.

Her voice lodged in her throat, Liz touched his hand and managed to say before the paramedics rolled him away, "You're going to be fine," even though she knew no such thing.

Chief Houghton waved the remaining crowd into the dining room. Everyone appeared to be in shock, and some of Helen's crew cried openly. Donita scurried around, trying to make sense of what her residents had done. Liz and Naomi stood silently, taking in the scene before them.

The chief glanced in their direction. "Are you two okay?"

"Yes." Liz's voice trembled when she spoke. "But I have to say, I'm not a fan of a gun being waved in my face."

"I'll second that," Naomi uttered.

The outrage Liz had forced herself to control finally made its way to the surface. She shot across the room, catching Helen off guard. "How could you keep a man against his will? Not to mention the heartache you caused Josh's parents and Renee."

"It was for a greater good," came her weak answer. If it was possible, Helen looked even older than an hour ago.

As the police straightened out the chaos, Liz called Mary Ann with an update. Once the shock wore off, everyone would be appalled at what Andrew and Helen had done. For now, they were happy to have found Josh. Mary Ann promised to immediately call Renee, so she could get to the hospital and be reunited with her fiancé. Her next call would be to Josh's parents.

Just then, Colonel Burns dragged Pete Hardy by the collar into the fray. "Caught him trying to escape."

"Hey, I want no part of this." Pete threw his hands up in surrender. "I'll tell you everything I know."

"Which is?" Liz asked.

The chief cleared his throat.

Liz gave him a sheepish grin. "Sorry."

"Okay, I wanted the seniors' money," Pete admitted. "But I had no idea they were keeping Josh locked up here."

"So you did Andrew's bidding?"

Pete looked away. "A few times. He controlled my money. I had no choice."

"No choice in tampering with my car?"

Pete's face colored. Was it from embarrassment? "I had to."

"And the judge's brakes?" the chief asked.

At this, Pete raised his head, eyes blazing. "He had it coming. I wanted to ruin him. Ruin his precious son's wedding." He clenched his fists. "Why should they be happy when I was in debt? The wedding was as good a place as any to make them pay."

"You dropped the crumpled invitation?" Liz whispered.

"Yeah. I swiped it from Josh's desk." When his spate of anger wore off, Pete realized his mistake. "I want an attorney."

"Gerst, take him to the station," the chief ordered. "Dixon, try to get statements from the rest of the crowd."

Liz turned to the chief. "At least we know what happened."

"What a mess," he murmured.

Someone called his name from across the room. He nodded to Liz and moved on.

Liz took a seat beside Naomi, who still wore a shell-shocked expression.

"You look the way I feel," Liz told her.

"I'm . . . there are no words."

They sat quietly, watching the proceedings in front of them.

Finally, Liz spoke. "No wonder I couldn't figure out what was going on. Who would have thought all three of the people I suspected of being involved in this actually were?"

"To be fair, you thought the entire senior center was in on it too."

"At first. Until I got to know some of them. And met Helen." Liz rubbed her forehead. "How could I have missed it?"

"Like you said, they were all involved in one way or another. Pete may have had different motives, but he played his part."

"What was Helen thinking, inviting Andrew into her scheme?"

"She wanted to outdo us," Betty said as she joined them. "She always thought she had the bigger, better ideas." She rested her cane against the table. "I swear, most of us had no inkling Josh was being held here."

"I believe you." Liz smiled at the older woman, her heart squeezing at the regret in Betty's eyes. "These past two weeks have been mind-boggling. I'm glad it's all over."

Naomi patted Betty on the shoulder. "Thanks for keeping an eye on things here."

"I'm only sorry I didn't catch on sooner." Betty bowed her head. "I'm completely in shock at what Helen and the others did. I can't believe one of our own would stoop this low."

"We owe you," Naomi said to Betty and the others who had moved closer. "Big-time."

The colonel awkwardly cleared his throat, then hung his head. "I'm going to have to give up my watch. I let you all down."

"You couldn't have known," Naomi assured him.

"But I should have. I was a scout in the army. I went ahead of the missions. Looked for problems. I missed a large problem here."

Liz touched his arm. "Which is?"

"I thought the room off the kitchen was a closet. But it turns out there's a door to the outside in there. It must have been used as a utility room at one time."

"So that's how Andrew and the women could come and go without being seen," Liz said.

The colonel tugged on his earlobe. "If only I had realized it sooner."

Naomi leaned forward. "If you don't mind my asking, how did you figure it out?"

"Pete. He was the one standing guard out front. Once I got a read on the situation in the kitchen, I slipped away and called the authorities. He tried to stop me, but I have many years of combat experience on my side. He took off and I followed, right to the outside door. If you didn't know it was there, you'd never notice it. There are two tall, overgrown shrubs on either side of the doorway and not much of a landing off the entry. It's nearly hidden." Colonel Burns shoved his hands into his pockets. "I guess he thought he could sneak in and warn Andrew."

"So he did know about Josh?"

"I can't say. But he did know about the door."

"As did the others. They obviously used it to sneak around."

Everyone thought about the newest revelation for a long time. Then the dining room began to clear out.

Liz rose and said to Naomi, "We should get to the hospital. I'm sure Mary Ann and Sadie will be waiting."

"They'll be on pins and needles."

Liz smiled at the wonderful seniors she'd come to love. "Thank you all. You sure have made life interesting."

In a solemn tone, Curtis said, "Call on us anytime, Liz."

"What on earth for?" she teased. "Are there other schemes going on that I should know about?"

"Not right now but there probably will be soon." A charming grin curved his lips. "What can I say? We crave excitement. And at our age, that mostly means food."

21

When Liz and Naomi arrived at the hospital, they found Mary Ann, Sadie, Opal, and Caitlyn sitting in the waiting room. After Liz relayed the story of Josh's disappearance, Andrew's master plan, and Pete's part in the debacle, they stared at her in shocked silence.

Opal spoke first. "My goodness, that is quite a tale."

"I'm not surprised," Sadie said. "Why do you think I don't hang out with that crowd from the senior center?"

"Because you have a job?" Mary Ann queried.

"Well, yes, but those people are troublemakers. Mark my words, we haven't heard the last of them."

Despite what had happened at the center, Liz hoped Sadie's words weren't true.

"I've never had a gun pointed at me," Caitlyn mused. By the awe in her tone, Liz wondered if she was the tiniest bit disappointed she'd missed the action.

"Trust me, it is not pleasant. The way Andrew was pacing and ranting. . ." Liz shivered. "There was no reasoning with him. Honestly, it could have gone either way. But thankfully the police showed up right after Colonel Burns called them."

An hour passed as they sat together, waiting for an update on Josh's condition. They'd spent too much time wondering about his whereabouts; they weren't about to leave before learning how he was.

Finally, the Conrads entered the waiting room. The knot in Liz's stomach unraveled at their peaceful expressions.

Elyse went straight to Liz and gave her a big hug, then hugged Naomi. "I can't thank you enough for finding our son." She choked up for a moment. "He's going to be fine."

Relief flooded Liz.

The judge joined them, his face having regained the natural healthy color that had been missing during his son's disappearance. "The doctor says the effects of the sleeping pills will completely wear off by tomorrow or the next day. But he's dehydrated, and they're keeping him overnight for observation and to give him fluids."

"I'm so happy this all worked out," Liz said. "For everyone."

"If it hadn't been for your relentless searching—" The judge stopped and cleared his throat. "Josh might not be with us."

"But he is. We have plenty to celebrate."

"We wanted to give Josh and Renee some time alone, so we're going to get coffee." Elyse's face brightened as she regarded her new friends. "Care to join us?"

Liz glanced at the other women, recognizing the collective answer. "No thanks. You two go on."

Before they left, the judge took his phone out of his pocket. "I'm going to get an update from the chief. I'll keep you in the loop."

"Thanks," Liz said as the couple exited the room arm in arm. She could only imagine the mess the chief had to untangle.

Mary Ann leaned back in her chair. "I don't know about you, but I'm exhausted."

"Typical response after extreme stress," Caitlyn informed them. "The body needs to rest."

"Which we should do after all this worrying," Sadie agreed. "I say we go home. Let the kids spend time together."

The women were in the process of gathering their purses and coats when Renee came into the room. She still looked haggard, but her smile was bright. "Leaving so soon?"

Mary Ann walked over to give her goddaughter a quick hug. "We heard the good news. Josh is going to be fine."

"Yes." Renee ran a hand over the back of her neck. "This whole ordeal has been horrible, but he's back. I feel like I can breathe again."

Liz placed a hand on her arm. "We're happy you two are back together where you belong."

"It never would have happened without your help. Thank you."

"Shouldn't you be with Josh?" Caitlyn asked. "If it was me, I'd be glued to his side."

"Oh, I'm going back in, but Josh wants to see you before you leave."

Opal raised her brows in confusion. "All of us?"

"All of you."

Surprised, Liz asked, "Are you sure? He needs to rest."

"He wants to thank you personally." Renee hooked her arm through Liz's and led the way to Josh's room. They entered to find him reclined in the partially raised bed, eyes closed.

"I'm back," Renee announced.

Josh's eyes fluttered open. He blinked a few times before a slow grin appeared. "The gang's all here," he said, his voice scratchy. He cleared his throat and shifted awkwardly.

Renee hurried over, positioning the pillow behind him and taking a seat on the edge of the bed. She clasped his hand.

"I owe you," Josh said to the group, his voice clearer.

"It's because of your fiancée," Mary Ann told him with motherly affection. "She put us on the job as soon as you vanished."

"And for that I'll be eternally grateful." He lifted their joined hands and kissed Renee's palm. "I understand I missed most of the excitement."

"Sleeping pills will do that to a person," Sadie said as she took a seat in the empty chair.

"I still can't believe . . ." His voice wavered.

Liz stood beside the bed. "What on earth happened?"

"It all started with the loan." Josh dropped his head back onto the pillow.

"W&K Quality Merchandise and Manufacturing?"

Josh nodded. "On the surface, it seemed like just another business loan. But as I started going over the application and the information they supplied me, I realized something was off. I researched the company and discovered they were on the verge of bankruptcy, but the numbers they gave me didn't reflect the problem. I went to Fairfield with my concerns, and he told me to do my due diligence. So I nosed deeper. I got the underwriter involved earlier than I normally would have to get to the truth. I even sent a request to the IRS for past tax returns."

Liz tilted her head. "The night of the rehearsal dinner, who were you talking to?"

"The underwriter. We still had a few dots to connect, and I didn't want to go on my honeymoon until we figured them out."

"Why visit Caleb the morning of the wedding?" Sadie asked as she moved to the edge of her seat.

"Nerves. Here I was on the most important day of my life, and my attention kept going back to a loan I knew we were going to deny. I felt guilty." Josh glanced at his fiancée, love shining in his eyes. "Renee had put her heart and soul into our special day, and I was distracted. On top of that, my dad and I had argued the morning of the wedding. Going out to Caleb's farm has always been a stress reliever for me, and I drove out there early to find some peace. I needed to get my head together, so I could focus on Renee and the big day."

Renee leaned over and placed a tender kiss on his cheek.

"I was driving back to the inn for the wedding when the underwriter called me. He had the last piece of the puzzle. Not only were we going to deny the loan, but because of the false numbers they gave us, we were going to report them to the authorities."

"How did you get kidnapped?" Caitlyn blurted.

"And how in the world was Andrew involved?" Opal asked at the same time.

"It's kind of a long story," Josh said. "I knew Andrew and I would be competing for the loan. It seems like we always do. Early in the process, as I started to have my doubts about the validity of the company, I called Andrew to warn him as a professional courtesy and left it at that."

"What happened then?" Naomi inquired.

"Andrew left a message on my phone while I was talking to Caleb," Josh continued. "I returned his call after I spoke to the underwriter. He said he had an important document that would prove the company was giving us false numbers. Said he was at his office and if I swung by, he'd give it to me and I could be on my way. I told him I'd stop outside, and he could run the paper out to me. When he came to the car, he handed me the paper. I started to read it, totally distracted."

Renee squeezed his hand, encouraging him to go on.

Josh made a face. "I never noticed the cloth in his hand. Must have had chloroform or something on it. When he tried to place it over my mouth, we struggled. The next thing I knew, I woke up in a strange room with two older ladies forcing tea down my throat. From then on it was a blurry haze."

"And the blood on your seat?"

"I'm guessing I got cut when Andrew yanked me from the car." He lifted his arm to show them a long, jagged cut. "Doc said it was deep, but the ladies at the center must have bound it up so I don't need stitches."

Mary Ann fanned her face with her hand. "Thank goodness. We were worried sick."

"It looks worse than it really is."

The women fussed over him until Liz returned to the topic at hand. "Did Andrew know the company was in trouble?"

"Not too long ago I would have said yes, but after what he did to get me out of the way, I'm not so sure. He must have thought he could finesse the system and get what he wanted." Josh set his gaze on Renee.

"He never would have gotten me," she whispered.

Pulling his gaze from Renee, he asked the group, "How did you find me?"

"It was all Liz," Naomi said.

Liz explained the hoops she'd jumped through to uncover the truth.

When she finished her story, Josh appeared even more dazed. "Unbelievable."

"What is unbelievable is how far Andrew and Helen were willing to go to attain their goal."

"Told you to watch out for her," Sadie sniffed.

"I guess I can understand Andrew wanting to woo Renee. But the rest?" Josh rubbed his head. "It's right out of a movie."

Renee stood. "Are you okay, Josh?"

"Just tired." He laughed. "Which is ironic after being forced to take sleeping meds."

"We should go," Liz said. "We'll have plenty of time to catch up later."

The doctor came in, eyes wide at the number of visitors in the room.

"That's our cue to leave," Caitlyn said as she greeted the doctor.

After getting a positive prognosis, the women filed from the room. It had been a long two weeks, but Josh was alive and well, and that's all that mattered.

———— *//////////////////////////////////* ————

Josh was released from the hospital a day later. He and Renee decided to get married right away, even if they wouldn't have the big wedding Renee had wished for. They were thrilled to be reunited and wanted nothing to stop their happy union. They chose the following Saturday for the wedding. Three weeks after he'd vanished, they would recite their vows with close family and friends assembled in the library at the inn.

Chief Houghton stopped by the inn to give Liz an update. Andrew had tossed Josh's phone on the county road to keep police guessing. Pete had admitted to cutting the brake lines on the judge's car in the name of payback and, on Andrew's order, tampering with Liz's vehicle to keep her from snooping around. Finding Josh's car on his property had spooked Pete enough to act without asking questions, especially when he found out Andrew was the one who had hidden the car. Discovering blood had made Pete even more fearful of what Andrew might do or try to pin on him.

As for Andrew, Helen, and their accomplices, sedating and keeping Josh against his will would cost them more than they had anticipated.

Liz had a week to get ready for the wedding, on top of hosting guests, but she took time out of her busy schedule to throw a tea party for Grace. The young girl had finished the quilt and couldn't wait for Liz to see it.

Liz set Wednesday as the unveiling day, and she had tea and cookies ready in the sitting room when Miriam arrived with Grace and Keturah. After they were seated on the couch, Grace removed the finished quilt from the basket she'd carried it in.

"Grace, this is beautiful."

The girl colored but didn't hide her grin.

"I helped too," her little sister added.

"Keturah," her mother admonished.

Liz laughed. "It's okay, Miriam. I know it was a Borkholder family effort. I love it."

"Where are you going to put it?" Keturah asked.

Glancing at Grace, Liz said, "Any suggestions?"

"It is your home. You should place it anywhere you please."

"I thought it would look good here," Liz said, indicating one of the walls. "I took down the pictures last night to make room for it." She held the quilt up against the wall. "Are we in agreement?"

Keturah clapped.

"I'll take that as a yes."

Liz took her seat and carefully folded the quilt, then patted Grace's knee. "Thank you again."

As the girls sipped tea and giggled, Miriam leaned over to Liz. "With the many preparations you have for the wedding, you did not have to invite us over today."

"I wanted to. If I learned anything these past couple of weeks, it's that I will never take my loved ones for granted."

———————— ⁘⁘⁘⁘⁘⁘⁘⁘⁘⁘⁘⁘⁘ ————————

The rest of the week passed in a blur. Saturday morning dawned cold but sunny. A sense of excitement permeated the inn. Today Renee and Josh would finally be married, and Liz vowed nothing would get in their way.

The Material Girls arrived early to decorate the library and dining room. They'd managed to get the florist to re-create the original flower order, and the caterer was more than happy to make lunch on a much smaller scale this time. Naomi baked a smaller version of the wedding cake.

The women had all donned their finest dresses, Sadie sporting a wide-brimmed hat the same burnished-copper color as her dress. Liz had even found a ribbon to tie around Beans's neck for the festive occasion.

At noon, the couple stood at the head of the room, Renee in her wedding gown with the Conrad brooch once again fastened to her waistline, and Josh in his tux, reciting vows that held so much more significance after what they had endured. Sadie happily snapped pictures with her phone. Mary Ann wiped away a tear when Pastor Brad pronounced them husband and wife. With a whoop, Josh took Renee in his arms and twirled her around before planting a well-earned kiss on her lips. The crowd clapped at his exuberance.

Shortly before the couple was to leave on their honeymoon, Mary Ann summoned the Material Girls and Renee to Sew Welcome. The shop was closed for the day, but she wanted to give Renee her wedding gift away from the others.

"Are you sure?" Renee glanced over her shoulder, as if afraid to leave Josh's side.

"Humor me."

"We actually planned to pull you away from Josh at the last, er, gathering," Sadie said. "Until everything changed."

Renee threw her hands in the air. "Okay then. I can't wait to see what it is you're all excited about."

Caitlyn removed the big box from behind the counter and set it on the cutting table. Everyone gathered around in expectation.

"It's lovely," Renee whispered.

"It'll be better when you open it," Sadie urged.

Chuckling, Renee carefully pulled the tape free and removed the wrapping paper. She took off the lid and folded back the decorative tissue, gasping when she glimpsed the quilt nestled inside. She gently took hold of it and withdrew it from the box. "It's a picture of Josh and me."

Mary Ann circled her arm around Renee's waist. "We wanted to give you a special gift, one you'd always remember."

"Trust me, I'll never forget either of my wedding days." Renee examined the quilt for a long moment and tilted her head. "Is this material from when I was a kid?"

"Yes. I kept a box of fabric after your grandmother passed. I knew one day it would come in handy."

Renee reverently ran a finger over the quilt blocks, her eyes bright with unshed tears.

"Elyse donated some of Josh's clothing," Liz pointed out. "We knew combining both of your pasts to make this quilt would be the finest gift we could give you."

Renee looked up and met each woman's eye as a tear escaped her own. "It's beautiful, especially since I know how much love went into stitching this special quilt. Thank you."

The women chatted a few minutes longer until Josh popped his head in the door. "Ready to go? Our flight leaves in a few hours."

"Oh gosh, yes." Renee wiped her damp cheeks.

Liz closed the box. "This will be here when you get back."

"Hurry now." Mary Ann shooed the bride to the door. "You don't want to miss your honeymoon."

"No chance of that happening." Renee grinned at Josh. "Now that we have our happy ending."